"Maybe you're not such a bad influence after all, Tess."

Mason laughed, amazed that Tess had talked him into swimming in the ocean…with his clothes on, no less. What was even more amazing was that it felt good.

"Me? A bad influence?" She kicked closer to him, until the warmth of her body surrounded him and her lips hovered over his. "Never."

His gaze fastened on her mouth. He swayed closer to her. Laughter from a group farther up the beach grew loud.

"Maybe we should head out of here." Mason pushed away from her, toward the shore.

A seductive smile curved her lips. "But you were going to kiss me."

"Was I?"

"Yes, you were. I saw it in your eyes." She tilted her head in a familiar gesture. "What's wrong? Too stuffy to kiss me in public?"

"Nope, just want some privacy." He swam closer to her. "Because when I kiss you again, I intend to enjoy the hell out of it."

Dear Reader,

Maybe it was because I grew up with four sisters, but as I developed Nikki's story in *The Morning After* (Harlequin Blaze #196) I was thrilled to discover that Nikki had sisters of her own.

Tess, my heroine in *So Many Men...*, came to me the strongest with her colorful personality and way with men. To me, she captured the free spirit so many of us bury beneath our more responsible roles. It was cathartic to let her run free, then rein her in as she grew to find a more fulfilling side to her life.

I hope you enjoy *So Many Men...*, where love heals all. Look for Erin's story, *Faking It,* the final installment of SEXUAL HEALING, coming in October 2005.

As always, it's a pleasure to share my stories with you. Feel free to write me at dorie@doriegraham.com or P.O. Box 769012, Roswell, GA 30076. Also, please visit my Web site at www.doriegraham.com.

Best wishes,

Dorie Graham

Books by Dorie Graham

HARLEQUIN BLAZE

*Sexual Healing

SO MANY MEN...
Dorie Graham

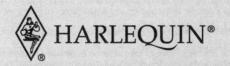

TORONTO • NEW YORK • LONDON
AMSTERDAM • PARIS • SYDNEY • HAMBURG
STOCKHOLM • ATHENS • TOKYO • MILAN • MADRID
PRAGUE • WARSAW • BUDAPEST • AUCKLAND

I dedicate this to my Georgia Romance Writers writing sisters.
Each of these women has contributed in some way to my growth and
success as an author: Adrianne Byrd, Anna DeStefano, Donna Sterling,
Carmen Green, Stephanie Bond, Patti Callahan Henry, Rita Herron,
Karen Kendall, Tanya Michaels, Patricia Lewin, Heidi Umbhau,
Rachelle Wadsworth and Ann Howard White, as well as all the ladies in
the Georgia Romance Authors Network and so many others I don't have
room to list. I am eternally grateful for your friendship and support.

ISBN 0-373-79206-9

SO MANY MEN...

Copyright © 2005 by Dorene Graham.

This edition published by arrangement with Harlequin Books S.A.

www.eHarlequin.com

Printed in U.S.A.

1

How MANY MEN COULD one woman handle? Tess McClellan inhaled a deep breath as the Miami Dolphins scored a touchdown on the TV and chaos erupted around her. A dirty gym sock flying by her head and the ringing of the doorbell added to the commotion, drawing loud hails for the pizza deliveryman.

"Sorry, Tess, I was aiming for Ramon." The owner of the sock grinned sheepishly at her.

Tess shook her head and extricated herself from the couch, amid the objections of no less than three of her male companions who were using her as a pillow. She glanced around at the group of men, all her ex-lovers. She had loved each one heart and soul, loved them still in fact.

Why then this growing dissatisfaction?

"Where you going, sweetheart? The game's just getting good." Ramon, her most recent ex, tugged at her hand, urging her back to the couch.

"I…I need some fresh air."

"I'll come with you." He set down his beer, but she shook her head.

"Don't get up. They're starting again." She nodded toward the TV. "I'll be right back."

"You sure?" Ramon asked, but his attention had already riveted back to the action on the screen.

Tess sighed. Lately, this need for distance from her minions, as her sisters had dubbed her collection of men, gnawed at Tess more and more. She let her gaze drift over the half-dozen men sprawled around her living room. They'd do anything for her. She had but to insinuate a need and they fought over who would fulfill it, whether it be picking up her dry cleaning, cooking her dinner or fixing her broken toilet. And this was only half of them.

What woman would complain?

"Hey, Tess, we're a little short on the pizza. Can you kick in?" Nate set a towering stack of pizza boxes on the coffee table already strewn with beer cans and half-filled bowls of chips. The men tore at the boxes with ravenous delight.

Tess glanced at the young Hispanic delivery guy standing wide-eyed by the door, then back at her own guys as they vied to see who could stuff an entire slice of pizza into his mouth first. Okay, maybe there was some reason for her dissatisfaction.

She turned to the newcomer. "Hold on just a second."

With a shake of her head she walked to her bedroom, reminding herself of all the good her guys had done for her lately. Just that morning, Ramon had stored a week's worth of meals in her freezer, Gabe had fixed the broken shelf on the bookcase in her bedroom, and Evan had finished scheduling her staff at the nursery for the upcoming week.

By the time she'd paid for the pizza she'd never eat, her heart swelled with warmth for all of them. Each one of them had been there for her, and if she needed them, they'd be there again. In a heartbeat.

The delivery guy nodded his thanks, then beat a hasty retreat. She stood in the door a moment and breathed in the heavy Miami air. The humidity still curled her hair, even this late in September.

Closing the door, she turned to her entourage. "I'm going out back to get a little air."

A couple of them bobbed their heads, but between the pizza and the game, they hardly seemed to notice her. She did a quick scan of them, assessing the various emotions each felt. They all seemed content to one degree or another.

All was well. That meant she'd done her job. And though no deep emotion currently ran through the group—other than for how the Dolphins were faring—she felt no concern. This was the way it always was—the lull between lovers.

She headed through the kitchen toward the back door, bent on a few moments of solitude on the shaded deck, even if it meant frizzing her hair in the remaining afternoon heat.

As she swept by the kitchen table, she grabbed the newspaper. Maybe she could see a movie. Of course, it wouldn't be as much fun by herself. Where was Erin? Her younger sister had made her presence way too scarce since their oldest sister, Nikki, had moved out.

"I don't need Erin," Tess assured herself as she settled in the padded lounger one of her guys had given her—she forgot which one—last year for her birthday. She opened the paper. "Now, what's going on in the world?"

But instead of the headline news, she'd grabbed the community section. She skimmed the list of upcoming events. Maybe she needed a little community involvement—a new charity to distract her. She hadn't volunteered for anything in quite a while. Maybe that was what was eating at her.

She scanned the options. United Way…Friends of the Elderly…Dade County Women's Club—a women's club? What did they do?—Make a Wish Foundation…"

She bit her lip. A women's group? That would mean no men. No testosterone, no dirty socks flying about, no paying for pizza she'd never eat…

Maybe that was what was troubling her—what this… emptiness in her life was. With her mother traveling abroad with her latest lover and her sisters tied up in their respective lives, was Tess merely craving female companionship?

But would she find friends in the Dade County Women's Club? A feeling of trepidation stole over her. Memories of high school flashed through her mind. She hadn't intentionally set out to date the head cheerleader's boyfriend, or the senior class president, or the star quarterback. She hadn't realized the power of her smile or even of an interested glance.

She hadn't known then that she had the McClellan gift of sexual healing.

The animosity of every female in school quickly had clued Tess in, though, that she was…different. As much as she'd tried, she couldn't make up for the continued interest of guys. She'd never had a girlfriend and, after a time, she'd given up. She'd had her sisters, after all, and she'd liked having so many male companions. And as she'd grown up, she'd enjoyed them as lovers.

But now something was wrong. The disquiet she'd experienced lately rippled through her. Did the women's club hold the answer to what was missing from her life? That group wouldn't have any men to distract her. Maybe she'd find acceptance among her female peers and she'd be giving to her community, something she'd always found fulfilling in the past.

She read the announcement again. There was a luncheon on Sunday—tomorrow.

Should she go?

"Josh, go long." A muffled yell filtered through the window, followed by a crash and the tinkling of broken glass.

She folded the paper and tucked it under her arm as she rose to investigate the latest upheaval in her home.

A testosterone-free afternoon.

How could she resist?

"ARE YOU SURE YOU WANT to do this?" Nate peered at her through the open car window, his dark eyes questioning.

She buckled her seat belt, then gripped the wheel, ignoring the tightening in her gut and the alarming urge to invite him along. She'd gotten way too used to having her own little entourage escort her everywhere. "I'm sure. I'll be fine. It's just a luncheon. Should be fun. I'll be back before you know it."

"Okay, Josh and I are going to hit a few balls on the courts." His shoulders eased in a slight shrug. "If you need anything, just call."

"I'll be fine," she reiterated, a nervous smile tugging at her lips. Was she reassuring him—or herself? "It's just a meeting of the Dade County Women's Club. What could happen?"

He stepped away from the car, frowning. "Not sure why you think you need to rub shoulders with those women, but knock 'em dead."

"Thanks, Nate. I should be back in plenty of time for dinner."

"We'll heat up one of Ramon's specialties."

The sun glanced off a bumper in front of her a short while later. A panhandler peered at her from a street corner, looking downtrodden and wearing too many layers of clothing in the heat. Her heart gave a little squeeze. She didn't have time now, but she'd bring him some food on her way back.

Lifting her chin, she gripped the wheel and focused on the road. She could do this. She'd walk into this meeting with her head held high. Without a man in sight she shouldn't have any problems striking up friendships with the club members.

A short time later, she took a deep breath as she pushed through the doors at the Hennesy Hotel. Soft music filled the lobby. She followed a sign and the murmur of voices to a meeting room. With her stomach flip-flopping and a smile plastered across her face, she strode into the room.

"Good afternoon, may I help you?" A petite woman sitting at a table inside the door greeted her.

"Um, yes, I'm here for a luncheon with the Dade County Women's Club."

"Are you a visitor?" A wide smile broke across the woman's face. "We're always excited to have new people."

"I saw your meeting announcement in the community calendar. I thought I'd come see what you were all about."

"Welcome. This is our monthly member luncheon, where we hold our meeting and enjoy visiting with one another."

"I think that I might be interested in joining, if that's okay." The words surprised Tess, even as they left her own mouth. She'd meant only to check them out.

"Of course it's okay. We'd love to have you." The woman extended her hand to Tess. "I'm Cassie Aikens, program chair."

Smiling, Tess pumped her hand. "Tess McClellan. I've never actually done anything like this before."

"Attended a luncheon?"

"Joined a women's group." She'd done it again—committed herself before she'd had a chance to think it through. Yet something about this woman encouraged Tess in a way she'd never hoped to be.

"It's a lot of fun. I'll introduce you to Terry Kingsley when she gets here. She's this year's membership chair."

"That would be great."

Another woman entered the room and greeted Cassie. Her gaze shifted over Tess, who smiled. The newcomer was an attractive woman, with every blond hair in place. Tess, with her tangle of red waves, couldn't help but feel a little tug of envy.

"Hi, April, this is—"

"Tess McClellan." Tess extended her hand.

"Tess has come to visit with us and maybe join our group," Cassie said, adding to the introduction.

"April Emerson. How nice to meet you."

"April's our president. This is her fifth year. We all love her so much, we won't let her step down."

April's shoulders relaxed and the smile she directed at Cassie seemed genuine. She handed Cassie a crisp twenty-dollar bill. "It smells wonderful, Cassie. Did you order the chicken amandine?"

"With asparagus and those seasoned potatoes you like." She handed April her change, along with a ticket-like receipt.

April glanced around at the tables of chattering women. "Looks like almost everyone's here. We should start soon. I think I'll go get my food and sit."

"We're missing Terry. I want to introduce her to Tess, so we can get her signed up. We haven't had a new member in a long while."

April's gaze again swept over Tess. "No, we haven't." Turning abruptly, she addressed Cassie. "Why don't you finish up, then get your own food? I'd like to get started on time for a change."

Cassie frowned. "Sure. I guess I'm pretty hungry. If Terry comes, she can find me."

April left and Cassie shook her head. "She's normally more friendly. She's just going through a rough time right now."

"Oh. Here—" Tess pulled her wallet from her bag. "I need to pay. There will be enough food, right?"

"Don't worry about that. We always order a few extra meals for guests or speakers." Cassie took Tess's money, then handed her a receipt.

"Speakers? Who do you usually have?"

"Let's see, last month a couple of women from the Garden Society did a nice talk on indoor gardens. And today we possibly have someone from Project Mentor. They're on the schedule, but there's a chance they might not show." She shrugged. "It's a new nonprofit organization, run entirely by volunteers. They take the big brother-big sister thing a little further— Look at me running on. We should grab our food. April will start before we get through our entrées."

Closing the money box, Cassie motioned Tess toward several banquet tables laden with fresh bread, salads and serving dishes steeped in tempting aromas that made Tess's stomach growl.

The food tasted as heavenly as it smelled, almost as good as one of Ramon's creations. Tess swallowed a savory mouthful of the chicken and smiled as Cassie nodded in her direction. Her new acquaintance had led her to a table not far from the front, where a podium stood.

The women at her table had acknowledged her with cursory nods as Cassie had left to find a vacant seat nearby. Tess did her best to blend in as the women chatted to one another. She waited patiently for an opening in the conversation where she might add something witty or entertaining.

"Kevin is teething and he drools nonstop. Everything goes straight into his mouth and he soaks his little T-shirts right through, even though I keep a bib on him." The brunette to her left leaned toward the woman beside her.

Not much Tess could add there. Frowning, she focused on the plump redhead to her right. "Then Daddy said he had corns on top of his corns and he would *not* walk another step. I thought Mama was going to skin him, right there. I have never seen her so angry."

"Mmm, this asparagus is to die for," Tess commented to no one in particular.

The others continued discussing teething babies and parents with foot problems. How could she jump in on any of these conversations? They were all talking about families—*normal* families.

What did Tess know about that?

In near desperation, she glanced across the table to where two women sat in deep conversation. "And he hates school. Doesn't care for his teacher at all. It's a battle to make him go every day. He complains about everything. He won't do his homework. We have a teacher's conference scheduled this week and I just dread it."

Who was Tess kidding? She had nothing in common with these women. She could no more relate to their issues than they could relate to hers.

You see, I have this problem. I tend to collect men, first as lovers, whom I heal through sexual encounters, then as friends who stay on long after the loving. My sisters fondly call them my minions, because they do everything for me. I so much as hint at a need and it's filled. But they can't fill one of my most pressing needs— the need for female companionship. And though some may say that I do them all a great service in healing them, I feel I can do more to help my community. This is where you ladies come in.

Right, that would go over like a lead balloon. Why had she come? What made her think she could do this? Tess shook her head and looked over at Cassie. She waved and Tess relaxed a little. She'd made at least one connection, and that was better than she'd done all through high school and college combined. Maybe there was hope.

Cassie's gaze swung to the door, and her smile faded. A sudden taut silence filled the air and Tess turned to see April glaring toward the back of the room. Tess followed the glare to a dark-haired man, standing just inside the door.

He was solid, with a strong build and virile presence that rolled over Tess in waves. Her gaze traveled up his length to lock with his. His eyes and hair were a nondescript brown and his features more angular than she preferred, but still she was entranced and surprised at her own reaction. Certainly, catching a man's attention had never been a problem for her, but never before had she experienced this inexplicable draw. She braced her hands on the table and fought the urge to go to him.

Still, he held her transfixed and it took all her concentration to turn toward the front of the room. Her back ramrod straight, April moved to the podium, her expression heavy with censure as she glanced at Tess. A sense of bewilderment stole over Tess. What had angered April? Tess took a deep breath and struggled not to look at the man whose presence spiked the tension in the room.

The microphone came to life as April tapped it. "Excuse me everyone, I hope you've all had enough of this delicious meal. If not, please feel free to help yourselves to seconds. There's plenty."

She paused, but everyone remained seated, either with sated appetites, or apprehension over the obvious discord now present. She resumed speaking. "It seems we have a speaker who has arrived ahead of schedule, so I suggest we commence with that part of our program and leave the reading of the minutes and the business portion until later."

A murmur of assent rippled through the crowd. The redhead beside Tess raised her hand. "I move we save the minutes and business part of our meeting until after our speaker."

April smiled sweetly at the woman. "Thank you, Jen. Always nice to have you keeping us on track." She addressed the group. "Are there any seconds?"

Someone seconded the motion, then it passed with a unanimous vote. April cleared her throat. "So, with no further ado, here's Dr. Mason Davies to discuss his Project Mentor."

She walked stiffly to her seat as Dr. Davies strode up the aisle. He moved with a forceful grace, even though tension radiated from the tight set of his jaw and shoulders. He paused when he passed April's table. "Thank you."

April stared at him evenly, but made no comment as he continued to the podium. He adjusted the microphone, then let his gaze scan the room. "I'd like to thank you all for having me here today. I appreciate your time and consideration—especially your consideration. I won't beat around the bush. I've come here to ask for your help."

The low timbre of his voice vibrated through Tess, filling her with surprising swirls of awareness. His gaze again scanned the crowd, before coming to rest on her. Heat rose in her face as, spellbound, she couldn't look away.

Who *was* this man?

"For those of you who aren't familiar with Project Mentor, it's a program of volunteers working to help at-risk teens and children who have been exposed to drug abuse and/or HIV in their families. It's a nonprofit organization sponsoring workshops and other events designed not only to help relieve some of the immediate burdens these kids face, but also to help them plan for their futures.

"These kids are the unfortunate victims who fall between the cracks at school and in our communities. They struggle with issues no child should have to deal with, yet they live it. Some of these kids don't know what it's like to eat three square meals a day, have proper medical and dental care, or attend school on a regular basis. Many of them have given up by the time they reach us."

He paused. His passion for this project reached out to Tess and empathy swelled through her—for the children, for this man who cared enough that he faced this roomful of less-than-welcoming women. He and April certainly had some issues to work out. The pressure between the two of them was nearly a physical thing.

"What exactly is it that you're asking of us, Dr. Davies?" The question came from one of the women at April's table.

"That's an excellent question. Our hope is that you'll lend us a hand with some fund-raising."

"What kind of fund-raising?" another of April's group asked.

"That would ultimately be for you to decide, but at Project Mentor we had talked about a big gala or ball where the proceeds would go toward creating a youth center. We would, of course, welcome all youths, but our focus is on the ones we find through the free clinic we established two years ago in downtown Miami.

"Even though that clinic has experienced great success, we have seen more and more patients strung out on drugs and with HIV. When children are involved, our choice in the past has been to help the parents as best we could, then send them back to deal with their families as best *they* could. Unfortunately, they often don't deal well with the added pressure of raising children, especially teens.

"Though we have a mentoring program in place for these kids, we're finding it isn't enough. There's a real need to provide a feeling of community for them, a sense that they belong somewhere. If we don't supply that connection, they find it in gangs or other unfavorable settings. A youth center would help prevent that."

Tess glanced around expectantly, subduing the urge to jump to her feet and volunteer the group. She hadn't yet officially joined their ranks. So it wasn't her place to say anything. Surely, these women would put aside their differences for this higher purpose.

April straightened in her seat, though she remained closed off, her arms folded across her chest. "Why can't your group arrange this ball on its own?"

"You ladies are known for your fund-raising abilities. We could make an effort, but all of us have careers in addition to our volunteering with the project. We simply don't have the resources or connections you do. The gala is guaranteed success if the Dade County Women's Club is associated with it."

Silence reigned over the room. April uncrossed her arms and sat forward. "I don't see how we would have the time to help you. We have several other projects we're currently tied up with and our own gala event not far around the corner."

Disbelief flashed through Dr. Davies's eyes. "But that's nearly nine months away. Surely you'd have time to handle this event."

April rose, her eyes narrowed. "I don't think so. There's a lot that goes into planning any event as you so clearly point out, but I can't speak for the entire group." She gestured to the tables around her. "What do you think? Can we help Dr. Davies with his project?"

Tess stiffened at the note of warning in her voice. She held her breath as not a soul offered an opinion. How could these women just sit there? Did April swing so much clout that she could cow everyone into not helping?

Fisting her hands in her lap, Tess fought the urge to offer her services. She didn't even know these women. Why would they listen to her? Acting against April would most likely cost Tess any chance at making friends. And so much for service work with the group.

She glanced up to find his gaze on her and froze.

His dark eyes beseeched her. What could *she* do? Surely one of the other women would say something.

"I see." The defeat in his voice cut deep. "Then I won't be taking any more of your time."

Tess took another deep breath as he exited, but it did little to ease the knot of regret forming in her stomach. She stared at the empty doorway. The man had left. There wasn't anything she could do about it now. Besides, chances were another group would come to his aid. If he was a doctor, he must have all kinds of connections.

The women's club seemed to have other charities it

was involved in. Surely she'd find another project she'd feel good about helping with. And there was the added bonus of making women friends. She'd come here to get away from men. She sipped her water and tried to relax. With the good doctor gone, now maybe she could get on with building some kind of relationship with her own kind.

2

SHE WASN'T THEIR KIND. Everything about the redhead at the women's club told Mason Davies that she was cut from a different cloth. He closed his eyes against the image of the memorable woman who'd captured his attention. Though she'd sat in their midst, she was as different from those women as he was.

He'd seen the emotion shining in her blue eyes when he talked about the project. She'd understood the need—the fact that this event was worthwhile. Somehow, he had felt her dismay at the lack of support.

Yet, she'd sat silently as he'd left in defeat. He couldn't believe she was so like them. Something about her—maybe her bearing—seemed to say she'd made up her own mind about things, even though she'd held her tongue.

He shook his head. He needed to forget the redhead and focus on a new plan. She certainly wasn't giving his project—or him—any second thoughts.

Plastering a smile on his face, he continued down the hospital corridor to his next patient's room. Vases of flowers topped the dresser and nightstand. Peggy Williams was fortunate. Her husband had barely left her side since her arrival yesterday and it looked as though more family members had arrived today.

She smiled at him, only half her mouth lifting. He moved to the side of the bed. "Good morning, Peggy. How are you?"

She nodded slightly. "Um…ah…" She shook her head, frowning in frustration.

He glanced over her chart. "I see you ate better today. No problem swallowing?"

"Ah…um…no."

"Good." He paused to take her pulse.

"She ate a good bit of her lunch, though she had some trouble with the soup. Her hand was a little shaky and she kept spilling. I wanted to help her, but the nurse said that it was best to let her try on her own," Brad Williams explained.

"Soup?" Mason glanced at the lunch tray that had been pushed to one side. "That's great."

"This is our daughter, Paige, and her two girls, Leslie and Sarah." Brad gestured to the worried-looking brunette standing next to him and the two youngsters clinging to her sides.

"It's a pleasure." Mason smiled at the girls. A vibrancy and innocence that he saw in far too few children these days radiated from them. "I think it's helped your grandmother's spirits to have her family near. It's wonderful she has you to cheer her up."

He straightened and addressed both Brad and Paige. "The nurses were quite concerned yesterday that she seemed depressed. That can be tough on recovery. Having this kind of support can make all the difference to a patient."

"So what can you tell us, Doc? Will she recover?" Paige smoothed her daughter's hair.

"It's difficult to say. I don't want to give you any false hope, but the stroke was mild and it helped that your father brought her in right away. She's weak and recovery will take time. I'm referring her to a physical therapist as well as a speech therapist for her aphasia."

"Aphasia," Mr. Williams repeated. "That's her difficulty with her speech?"

"Yes."

"Is that why she can't tell us stories?" The smaller of the girls stared at him, wide-eyed.

"The language center of her brain was damaged, which isn't unusual in these cases. Your grandmother is as smart as she ever was, but it may take a little time before her brain rewires itself and she can tell you stories again."

"She has to learn to speak all over again?" Mr. Williams squeezed his wife's hand.

"Yes, more or less. The brain is a remarkable tool, though."

"She said 'hi' when we came in," the older girl said.

Her mother smiled at her, then turned to Mason. "When can we take her home?"

Mason glanced at his watch. Much of the day had already passed. "Let me see if I can get the speech and physical therapists in to check her out. We also need the social worker to see her and talk to all of you."

Mr. Williams glanced up. "Social worker?"

"It's standard. We need to be sure Peggy has all the support she'll require while she recuperates. We have to determine what kind of in-home care we need to supply. Once she's home she'll have a nurse checking on her—we'll decide how often and for how long. It's good that Peggy is eating without any difficulty."

Her husband nodded. "Can we take her home today? I know she'll sleep better in her own bed."

"We definitely want to get her home as soon as possible." Mason made a few notes, then returned the chart to its holder. "Let me see what I can do."

"Thank you, Dr. Davies."

As he headed to the nurses' station, Mason couldn't help but compare this family to the ones he met at the free clinic downtown. They were a world apart.

Regret flooded him. If only he'd been able to convince the women's club to help Project Mentor. Obviously, April was holding a grudge and she held all the clout with that group.

It was a damn shame.

"WHAT IS *WRONG* WITH YOU?" Nikki McClellan asked Tess Tuesday afternoon, as they strolled through the mall, shopping bags in hand.

Tess inhaled a deep breath. Why had she even mentioned Mason Davies to Nikki? Tess should have known her sister would react this way. Talk about ruining their time together.

"I'm sure he'll find someone else to help him. It *is* a worthwhile project," Tess said. "I'm not denying that, but it isn't as though he doesn't have resources of his own. He's got a whole organization with who knows how many volunteers. I don't see why he needed the DCWC anyway."

"DCWC?"

"The Dade County Women's Club."

"Tess, this is not like you. You can't walk by a home-less person without giving food or money. Are you telling me you sat there and said nothing while those women turned him down?"

"It wasn't my place to say anything. Terry Whatsit, the membership chair, never showed up, so I haven't even officially joined. How could I possibly speak for a group I'm not yet a member of?"

"For pity's sake, those kinds of details have never stopped you before. And since when are you keeping your opinion to yourself?" Nikki asked.

"I just expressed my opinion. It's a worthwhile cause."

"*I'm* not the one you need to be saying that to. I really cannot believe you didn't give the club an earful."

Frustration swelled in Tess. She hated Nikki's lectures, even when they were justified. "Maybe they know something about him that I don't. Maybe they have a solid motivation. There was definitely something off between him and April."

"For all you know they were having some kind of lovers' quarrel, and what in the world has that got to do with the fund-raiser?"

"Nothing. You're right. I should have spoken up, but…"

"But what?"

"They were *women,* okay? I'm used to women hating me. You know how it's always been. Why would they have listened to *me,* of all people? I'm an outsider. For once I just wanted to be…accepted." Even as she said the words, Tess cringed.

How pathetic was she?

Nikki crossed her arms and stared at her, eyebrows raised. "I hear that, Tess, but you know what you have to do."

Tess stared at her sister. Nikki had women friends. Did she understand that if Tess took on this project, she could kiss her plan to make her own friends goodbye?

"Okay...I'll go talk to this guy. At least check out this project in a little more detail." Tess shrugged. "No promises, but we'll see."

"YOU KNOW WHO'S USING and who isn't." Mason took a deep breath as he faced Rafe Black, one of the teens he'd recently met through the clinic. They stood in an open area around a fountain in the park near Mason's office. "You need to surround yourself with friends who aren't."

Rafe ran one finger along his eyebrow, where he had once worn a double stripe shaved at one end, a mark Mason feared showed the young man's allegiance to a gang, though he denied it. "But these are my boys, you know? Maybe I can help them. Maybe if they hang with me, then they won't use anymore."

"Or you could be tempted to use again."

"No way." Rafe stepped back in disgust. "I've seen what that shit did to my old man. No way is that going to happen to me." He thumped his chest. "I'm going to make something of my life, and if I can help some of my boys, then it's all straight."

"Will any of them come for the beach cleanup next Saturday?"

He shrugged. "I told them about it."

"Will *you* come? I'm happy to pick you up, if you need a ride."

"I can find my own ride."

He hadn't said he'd come. Even if he had, the odds

were against Rafe sticking with the program. Mason felt a flicker of disappointment. "Well, let me know if not. It's no trouble to swing by to get you on my way."

"It's all good. We'll see what's going down." Rafe stood, stretching his six feet two inches of lanky muscle, the lines of the man he'd become already evident. "I've got to head out."

Mason nodded. "We still on for some Hurricanes football?"

A wide smile spread across the young man's face. For just a moment the premature aging around his eyes faded and he appeared the carefree youth he should have been. He spiked an imaginary football. "Orange Bowl? You know I wouldn't miss it."

Hope filled Mason as Rafe sauntered down the path through the park. Maybe there was a chance he'd beat the odds, after all.

"He's lucky to have you."

Mason started at the feminine voice behind him. He turned, surprised to see the unforgettable redhead from the DCWC meeting.

"Hello." She extended her hand and smiled. "I'm Tess McClellan."

Inexplicable heat suffused him. His pulse raced. He stared at her, caught in the beauty of her smile until he belatedly grabbed her hand and pumped with more exuberance than necessary.

Pink rose in her cheeks. "I was at the Dade County Women's Club luncheon for your talk the other day."

"Yes, of course, I remember you."

Why was she here? He willed his pulse to calm and stuffed his hands into his pockets to prevent further spastic behavior. At twenty-nine he'd somehow become an awkward teen again.

"I hope you don't mind that I tracked you down. Cassie Aikens gave me your office number, and when I called, your receptionist told me I could find you here."

Muffled musical notes sounded from inside her purse. She dug a cell phone from it. "Excuse me a moment."

Turning aside she spoke in quiet tones to the caller. "Hi, Evan… I'm not sure… I'll be back later this afternoon… Ramon has dinner covered… I have to go… Okay, bye." She stowed the phone back in her purse. "I'm sorry about that."

"No problem. So, Tess, I assume you want to hear more about the project."

Up close, she was even more compelling than she'd been from a distance. Not exactly pretty—though the blue of her eyes was stunning—she was entrancing in an uncommon way. When was the last time he'd been this excited, this pleased, to see a woman—and one he didn't even know at that?

She smiled, revealing a small dimple in her left cheek, as she nodded. "I wanted to see for myself what it was all about." She pulled on her fingers—her ringless fingers. "I didn't want to disturb you, but I couldn't help but overhear your conversation."

"Rafe has had a difficult time, like so many of these kids. They each have a story—some born addicted to crack, some who've lost a parent to an overdose, some with HIV-infected parents, more times than not from needles they found in the trash." He shook his head. "It's hard to believe they don't know better. It's a pity to see people unable to care, especially with kids like Rafe counting on them."

"I can't even imagine."

Memories of his own childhood flashed through Mason's mind: the morning his mother took off without saying goodbye; his father drinking himself to death shortly afterward; being passed from uncle to uncle until he emancipated himself at sixteen. "Well, I never had it as hard as Rafe, but I can imagine."

Her gaze softened, and for a moment warmth seemed to flow from her, blanketing him in a sense of well-being. Unbidden, his feet moved him a step closer to her.

"So, you arrange activities for these kids to keep them off the streets?"

"That's part of it. We have regular workshops to educate them on drug abuse, HIV and other issues that affect them. Try to counsel them on school and careers and help them get jobs in the interim."

"Are most of them teens like that guy?" A breeze swept up behind her, bringing a whiff of her perfume.

His gaze fell to the fullness of her lips. Her scent teased him and he struggled to focus on their conversation. "We get them in all shapes and sizes. The teens are the ones we worry about the most, though. They're the most damaged. You can see it in the way they're closed off, distrustful of everything and everybody. Usually they're so close to falling off the edge, we're lucky to get any response from them."

"That's so…sad."

Something in her eyes pulled him in, held him spellbound for a moment, until he blinked and detached himself, inhaling a deep breath to clear his head. "Occasionally we get some of the more fortunate ones, latchkey kids being raised by single parents struggling with poverty and stressful lives. That's all part of the problem.

"Right now we're tapping all our resources to help the kids, but then we send them home to their parents, who are still saddled with all their issues. They can undo our efforts in the space of a day. If we can get this center going, we're hoping to start some new programs for parents and families as well."

Again she nodded, her forehead furrowed in thought. "And you think one big fund-raiser will be enough?"

"To be totally honest, I'd like this one event to help get us up and running. Then we'll need something similar at least annually to keep the center operating."

Her cell phone chimed again and she excused herself to answer it. "Josh, I'm so sorry I missed you... Can we do Sunday?... Great... Okay, I'm with someone, I have to go... See you then." After putting her phone away, she smiled at Mason. "I'm so sorry. Have you looked into getting grants and foundation money?"

"We're working on that, and hopefully our efforts will pay off. It's not a quick process, though."

"I'm sure." She remained silent a long moment and he waited as she paced around the area in front of the fountain.

Indulging himself, he drank his fill of the sight of her while she lost herself in thought. She was of medium height and weight, not too busty, not too flat. Hips that flared nicely and a decent ass. An average description for an extraordinary woman. What was it about her that made her so…appealing? It was more her presence—no, her essence—that drew him.

Just when he thought he could stand the silence no more, she stopped in front of him. "So," he couldn't keep from asking, "will you help us—help me?"

Her blue gaze locked with his and time seemed to suspend as something—a soul-deep recognition—settled over him. "Yes, Mason, I will rally the DCWC to help you. If they fail me, then I'll call on my own resources and do it myself."

A mixture of relief and excitement filled him. He pressed her hands in his. "Thank you, Tess. This means so much to me. I can't tell you how much I appreciate your support."

"I'm happy to help."

Tess cocked her head. Until this moment she hadn't been sure she was ready for another lover so soon—had thought she needed a little break—but she couldn't deny the proof standing before her. She could feel all that he felt, his gratitude, his excitement and, below that, growing stronger with their hands joined, the same heat sweeping through her. Something was different—she couldn't put her finger on exactly what. Certainly it was much more intense this time.

Still, this was how it always began.

This empathic rush was nothing new. She always knew what her guys felt. Not until recently, when Aunt Sophie had told her and her sisters about their gift, had Tess understood that her ability to feel others' emotions was part and parcel of her family heritage. Where Nikki had been able to tune into anyone around her, Tess's empathic nature worked only with her men.

Desire flowed off Mason in waves. There was no use in fighting it. His need, his pain, already called to her, buried deep inside him. She could no more turn away from him than she could stop breathing. She was a healer.

She would help him in so many more ways than he realized. First, though, she needed time with him, time to get to know him and gauge what troubles he harbored. She let her gaze travel up his arms and chest, over his strong features to his compelling eyes. Had she at first thought him nondescript?

No, this man had eyes that saw into the depths of her soul. A shiver passed through her. What could she deny him when he looked at her that way?

"So, how do you feel about coffee?" he asked. "I have some time before my afternoon appointments. Unless you need to be somewhere?"

"No, the nursery's covered. Coffee sounds great, though I can't stay too long. I like to be there when the shipment comes." She turned with him to head across the park to a nearby coffee shop.

"You work at a nursery?"

"Actually, I own it. I always liked plants and I have a green thumb. It made sense to buy the nursery when one of my great-aunts left me a small inheritance."

"Do you sell anything besides trees and flowers?" His lips curved into a smile.

She was going to enjoy kissing him.

"I have a nice assortment of stone statuary. And my sister is an interior designer so I am always special-ordering her something. Believe me, I can get you practically anything you want."

His eyebrows arched. His gaze dropped to her mouth and the desire simmering in him flared. "Anything?"

"That's right." She stopped walking and faced him. *"Anything."*

Heat arced between them. The intensity in his eyes held her breathless. She leaned toward him as he moved forward. A bird cawed overhead and suddenly he pulled away.

"You don't say?" he said, falling back into step. "I'll have to come by and see what you have. I've been meaning to do something with my front entrance, but haven't gotten around to it."

"I'm sure we can find something." She frowned as they crossed a small stretch of parking lot. Evidently, the man needed a little coaxing. "Maybe I should come see your front entrance sometime, so I can have a better idea of what you might need."

"Sure." He smiled again, and his pleasure, though guarded, reached out to her. "I think I'd like to have you over."

She threaded her arm through his and they entered the shop. The aroma of strong coffee drifted in the air. "It smells heavenly in here."

They ordered their drinks and Tess pulled her wallet from her bag. Mason raised his hand in protest. "I invited you. This is my treat."

"Thank you, but you'll have to let me treat the next time."

He pursed his lips as he held a chair for her. "We'll have to see about that. I believe a gentleman should always take care of a lady."

"You're kidding." She slipped into the seat and stared

at him as he settled opposite her. "I didn't know they still made them like you."

"They probably don't. I was raised kind of old school."

Once more, her cell phone summoned her. With a shake of her head, she pulled it again from her bag. "It's Max. I'll call him back."

She sipped her coffee, then smiled at Mason. "So, a man of convention."

He stared out the window overlooking the park. "I like the old values. If you could see half the trouble I've seen in some of the kids of today…" He shook his head and rolled his cup between his hands. "Just makes you wonder if the new ways of parenting are doing any good."

"I think it's hard to make generalizations."

"Perhaps."

His mood darkened and a short silence fell. She again sipped the rich brew. She'd have to ease him into meeting her family…or maybe avoid it altogether. "So I told you about my nursery. How about you? What sort of doctor are you?"

"I'm an internist. I specialize in the internal organs."

"You have a regular practice as well as the free clinic you mentioned?"

"That's right. We have a volunteer staff and we rotate the schedule, so I work only one day a week downtown and I'm on call for the free clinic one night. We have a couple of great general practitioners on staff, but the rest of us tend to specialize in one area or another. It means we consult back and forth a lot, so that adds in more hours. We're fortunate to have such a variety in our staff. It definitely strengthens the clinic."

"And you're able to juggle that with Project Mentor and your regular patients?"

"I have a couple of partners with my practice, who pick up my slack when I need them to. Of course, I've talked one of them into volunteering at the clinic and I'm working on the other. As far as the project goes, well, I try to make that a priority and fit it in as best I can."

"Sounds like you're always working."

"Seems that way sometimes. With my regular practice and the clinic I'm practically always on call, but I manage. Time with the kids isn't like work. We have some fun." He grinned. "Besides, I take long lunch breaks."

She leaned toward him. "Still, doesn't seem to leave much time for a personal life."

His gaze grew warm, his pupils dilating. "There hasn't been much going on there lately."

"Really? I heard you and April had a thing. That you two split up recently and that's why the cold reception at the DCWC." Cassie had filled Tess in on April's history with Mason as a way of explaining the club's refusal.

He straightened, his eyes widening. "You like to lay all the cards on the table, don't you?"

"I think it's important to keep the air clear. Should I extend my condolences?" Tess smiled inwardly. The air around him shimmered with surprise and a little regret, but no heartache. Whatever ailed him, it wasn't April.

He took a moment to sip his coffee. "Don't get me wrong, April is a wonderful woman and I had hoped for a while that we could have more in our relationship. It took me some time to figure out that that just wasn't going to happen. It wouldn't have been fair to either one of us to keep things going. We had let it linger for way too long as it was."

Tess reached across the table to touch his arm. The connection was strong, sending warm tingles over her. "I'm sorry."

"Nothing to be sorry about. People leave each other. Life goes on."

She shivered. Something dark and painful moved through him. Was that Mason's trouble? Had someone left him? "Mason—"

A beeper sounded from his side of the table. He blew out a long breath as he pulled a pager from his pocket. "Ah, here we go. Time to get back to work. I'm so sorry to have to cut this short."

She rose with him. "No problem. I need to get back myself."

They moved toward the door and he touched her elbow. "Thank you, Tess, for everything—the coffee, the company, offering your help. I just know good things will come of this."

They stepped through the door, then out into the parking lot. "Oh, definitely. Why don't I make a few calls to get the ball rolling? Then I'll be in touch to arrange a meeting so we can start organizing everything."

He smiled with genuine pleasure. "That sounds really great. Here, let me give you my contact info." He pulled a card from his wallet. "Have you got a pen?"

"Sure." She found a pen bearing her nursery's logo. "Here, keep this and you'll know where to find me most days."

"Great." His brows arched. "No home number?"

"My cell's on there, but anyone at the shop can get me if I'm not around."

He scrawled some more numbers across the back of his business card, then handed it to her. "That's my home phone, cell phone and pager. So now you have every means of reaching me. If you can't get me on one of those, I'm probably with a patient. Leave a message and I'll get back to you as soon as I can."

"So many numbers. I feel important."

"You are." The heat returned to his eyes. "I want you to be able to reach me whenever you need me, even if it's after hours."

She cocked her head, smiling. Was the good doctor actually flirting with her? That was definitely a good sign. "Trust me, I'll be in touch."

He squeezed her hand and nodded. "I'm really looking forward to it."

His pager sounded again and she shooed him away. "Go. We'll talk soon."

Nodding, he moved off, his cell phone already to his ear. The sun shone down on him, picking out vibrant streaks of auburn in his dark hair. She smiled as he turned to wave. Even across the parking lot, his excitement called to her. Maybe the good doctor wouldn't need so much coaxing, after all.

3

"BUT, CASSIE, HOW COULD you *not* want to do this?" Tess bit the inside of her lip. She knew she shouldn't push too hard, or she might lose any possible support from the woman. And if Tess was going to make it into the DCWC, she needed an ally on the inside. At least Cassie had been open to her stopping by her home when Tess had called to say she had something important to discuss.

Surely that was a good sign.

"It isn't that I don't agree that Project Mentor is a worthwhile project." Cassie's eyes took on a dreamy quality. "Anything Mason Davies is involved with is bound to be a huge success...."

"But? I definitely hear a *but* after that."

"But...April really won't like it. She's a good friend and we go way back." Cassie paused as if considering her next words. "There was more to it than I said before. They were engaged."

"April and Mason?" Though she'd suspected their relationship wasn't casual, hearing it confirmed was a bit of a kick to the gut.

"It was a long, drawn-out thing. Four years. How could anyone be engaged that long and not set a date?

I always thought there was something wrong there, but April never seemed to mind—always made excuses. I think finally even she got tired of waiting and put her foot down. That's when he dumped her."

"*He* called it off?"

"Well, she says it was mutual, but if that's the case, why is she so mad at him? Seems otherwise she'd just go on with her life and be glad it was over with. Don't you think?"

"When did all this happen?"

"Early last week. I called him Friday to see if he was still coming to the luncheon—he'd been on the agenda for months. I really thought that he would back out under the circumstances." She shook her head. "But not Mason. You have to admire him for that. It was kind of like facing a firing squad."

"Did April know he would be there Sunday?"

"I told her. She said he wouldn't show. That he would know better."

"But he did show."

"And she shot him down."

"Yes, she did."

Cassie leaned toward Tess. "But that wasn't really April. She's just not herself right now. If you go ahead with this plan to help him, you'll risk making an enemy of her and possibly some of the other women in the club. She has a very loyal following."

"Even though she's holding a personal grudge and he's supporting a cause that's transforming the lives of children?"

"She's not so bad, you know. I can only imagine what she's going through, losing a man like Mason.

She's put her heart and soul into this organization and she's good at what she does. She really does care about the community." She frowned. "I've never seen her let a personal issue cloud her judgment like this."

"I don't have to do this with the DCWC. I understand that Mason likes the clout the group can give him and the project's success is practically guaranteed with it, but I have plenty of resources of my own." Her ex-lovers certainly gave new meaning to the term *manpower.*

"You do?"

Tess nodded. "I can't explain it, but I really want to be part of this club. I know if I join, then take on this project, I may be making more enemies than friends. But if I can make just *one* new friend in the process, it'll be worthwhile. And if not…well, I'll know I did the right thing by trying." She shrugged. "Besides, Project Mentor needs our help more than I need new friends."

"Oh, that's really sweet." Cassie's eyes narrowed and she chewed her bottom lip as though thinking about Tess's plan. "You would have a hard time pulling this off on your own."

Tess held her breath and waited.

"We've always followed April because she usually makes the best decisions, but in this case…" Cassie's gaze held Tess's. Excitement sparkled in her eyes. "Tell you what, let's go see Terry to get you on board as an official member. Then what would you say to you and I paying April a visit?"

"I'd say that's a plan."

"I'LL HAVE THE ROAST BEEF on whole wheat, hold the mayo, no pickle and a small house salad, ranch dressing on the side." Mason handed the waitress his menu that Friday afternoon, then turned to Tess, who sat across from him, flanked by Cassie and a man named Josh—a friend of Tess's.

The man hovered over Tess in an annoyingly territorial manner. Try as he might, Mason couldn't stem the irrational jealousy he felt as Josh draped his arm across the back of her seat. Mason frowned. Good God, he *had* turned into a hormonal teenager.

Tess smiled, her eyes shining as she glanced over the menu, seeming to take great pleasure in the simple act of ordering her meal. "I'll have some of that shaved blackened chicken on pumpernickel rye—" her gaze flicked to Mason "—load on the mayo, lettuce, tomato and pickles…lots of pickles. I'll have that with onion rings and the Caesar with the shrimp and…a loaded baked potato."

While their waitress took Josh's order, Mason stared in wonder. "You can't possibly eat all of that."

"I'll put a good dent in it. Josh gave me a good workout this morning. I'm starved."

Ha. Just as he'd suspected. Mason eyed Tess's *friend* as his jealousy stepped up a notch. Some friend.

The man was groomed to the max, from his perfectly styled hair to his buffed nails. He was built like a linebacker, with straight, honest features. April would have jumped him in a minute. A picture of Tess's *workout* flashed through Mason's mind and he stifled the image, frustrated that he should even care about this woman's romantic liaisons.

Tess McClellan was a sensual woman, and he couldn't deny a definite attraction. Her sex life was none of his business, though, even if fantasies of her had haunted him since their meeting at the park earlier in the week. After his disaster with April, the last thing Mason needed—or wanted—was to rush into another relationship.

Not that Tess was remotely his type.

Her cell phone rang and Mason did his best not to eavesdrop as she murmured consoling words to some guy named Kyle. She'd put her hair up into a kind of twist, but loose curls had escaped to fall around her face and the nape of her neck, giving her a wild, un-tamed look. Mason fisted his hand against the surpris-ing urge to touch one of those curls, to pull the clip free and run his hands through those glorious red waves.

He gave himself a mental shake. What was wrong with him? Normally he went for a more...conventional type of woman. Tess McClellan certainly didn't fit that bill.

"Mason, what time does it start?" Josh's question pulled him from his reverie.

Mason turned to him and blinked. "I'm sorry, what time does what start?"

A knowing smile broke across the man's face. "You know, you can't fight it, bro."

"Excuse me?"

Josh cocked his head in Tess's direction. "She's like magic—"

"Oh, look. Here's our food. That was quick. Thank goodness. I'm famished." Tess beamed as their waitress approached, her arms laden with dishes. Another server trailed after her, his arms also full.

The dark-haired server peered around their waitress as she bent to place the dishes on the table. "Tess?" he asked, his eyebrows arched in enthusiasm. "Hi, sweet-heart. I didn't know you were coming in today. Why didn't you tell me?"

"Mark, it's so good to see you." She raised her cheek as he placed a quick kiss there. "Since when do you work at this location? I thought you were in Hallandale."

"They had a staffing crisis. I'm filling in for a few days." He glanced around the table at the notepads and pens. "You having some kind of meeting?"

"We're working on a fund-raiser."

"Let me know if you need any help." He turned to Josh as he handed the dishes to their waitress. "How's it hanging, Josh? Haven't seen you in quite a while. Heard I just missed you at the apartment the other night when I stopped by to see our girl. You know how it is. I get the Tess jones on—"

"Mark, this is Cassie Aikens, with the Dade County Women's Club, and Dr. Mason Davies, with Project Mentor. We're trying to help Mason's group build a special youth center," Tess interrupted him.

Mark's eyes lit with understanding. "Right. Travis was telling me about that."

"Travis is back?" Tess and Josh asked in unison.

"He called the other night while you were busy with Jack. Kyle mentioned it to him."

Travis? Jack? Kyle? And all those calls. Who were all these men? And what were they to her?

Before Mason could form a coherent comment she waved her hand as if brushing aside his unspoken ques-tions. "More friends."

Mark bade her goodbye, with the promise to catch up with her later. After he'd left she turned back to

Mason. "We were talking about the beach cleanup next Saturday. What time does it start?"

"Are you *all* coming?" he asked, squelching the image of Tess surrounded by a flock of men.

Josh leaned forward. "I've already got a full schedule that day." He winked at Tess. "But Tess can round up—"

"I'm sure they have plenty of volunteers." Tess smiled stiffly.

Mason settled back in his seat. "Oh, we can always use more volunteers."

Josh opened his mouth, but Tess cut him off. "Cassie and I thought we'd lend a hand...if you need us and we won't be in the way."

"I would be more than happy to help," Cassie said. "Maybe we can round up a few of the others from the DCWC."

"Sure. We're glad to have you. We'll be at North Beach at nine-thirty."

"Tess?" A bearded stranger approached their table.

"Hi, Hugh." Her eyes widened, but she smiled and rose to exchange an enthusiastic, if brief, hug with this new man. "How are you?"

Cassie turned to Mason. "She certainly has a lot of *friends.*"

"That she does." Mason glanced questioningly across the table at Josh.

He shrugged. "She's *very* special."

"When did you get back into town?" Tess asked the latest arrival.

"Just this morning. I was passing by and saw you through the window. I was going to stop by the nursery, but looks like you won't be there."

"I've hired another full-time person. It's great. I can get away a little more often now. I'd love to hear about your trip some time, but we're in the middle of a meeting." She made introductions, then explained briefly about the fund-raiser.

"Hey, I can hook you up with an orchestra if you'd like," Hugh offered.

After Tess assured him she'd let him know, he gave her a quick kiss, then left, much to Mason's relief. Mason hated to admit it even to himself, but he might have to protest if one more man dropped by with a friendly hug or kiss for her. He shook his head, irritated with himself. He'd only just met the woman.

Why should he care?

He squelched the memory of the heated moments they'd shared in the park and over coffee. It wasn't as though anything had actually happened between them. He would *not* fall under whatever seductive spell she seemed to weave over the male population. That was the last thing he needed.

Though Tess's cell phone rang a few times, apparently with calls from more of her *friends,* they managed to make it through the rest of the meeting. From time to time Tess tossed in more names as resources for various aspects of the project. Whatever the need, be it advertising to catering, her connections seemed endless and all of them male.

"I'll go ahead and put these names and numbers in my database." Cassie scribbled a few more notes. "We'll see who can work us the best deals between our usual people and your…ah…friends, Tess."

Tess nodded, her mouth set in a firm line. "So, we

have our to-do lists. We've assigned tasks and set our priorities. Cassie, you're going to check on ballrooms and get back to us, so we can pinpoint locations and maybe a date." She paused, but no one added anything. "Should we set our next meeting time?"

They agreed to meet the following week. Josh offered to help Cassie carry out a file case she'd brought that held information from previous fund-raising events she'd helped coordinate for the DCWC. She and Josh moved off ahead of Tess and Mason, absorbed in conversation as Tess scooped up her large to-go container.

Mason glanced at her as they headed toward the door. His arm brushed hers and the heat she seemed to invoke in him rose. He cleared his throat and forced his gaze from the curve of her breasts. "Thanks for coming and rounding up the troops. This thing is sure to be a hit with the DCWC backing it. I don't see how we can miss with their expertise and your connections."

"It'll be great. You'll have your youth center."

"Tess!" Someone called to her from a table near the door.

Pink tinged her cheeks as she turned to greet what appeared to be yet another male admirer. Mason hung back as the man granted her the customary kiss and embrace. Something about the interaction spoke of an intimacy he refused to contemplate.

Exactly what sort of woman was he getting involved with? Not that they were *involved,* really. *If* he were looking for another relationship, it would be with a woman of a more…innocent nature.

"Another friend," she explained when she returned to his side.

"Tess, I hope you don't mind, but I just have to ask…" He held the restaurant door for her and Miami's heat blew over them.

She stepped past him into the bright sunlight, turning to him as they cleared the threshold. The breeze brushed over her, conforming the thin fabric of her dress to her curves. "Sure, ask me anything."

He focused on her eyes. "How *do* you know all those men?"

"You mean, are they really all just friends?"

"Yes."

"The answer is yes. They really are all just friends… now."

"Now?"

Her gaze locked with his. The same breeze stirred her curls. One shining wisp clung to her lip. "At one time— each in his own time—they were all my lovers."

"Oh." A buzzing sounded in his ears. His blood warmed and his body swayed toward her.

"Each in his own time."

"Yes, I got that." He swallowed. What was he supposed to say? He was having a hard enough time just breathing. The thought of her with all those men was at once both disturbing and oddly exciting.

The essence of her femininity flowed over him, drawing him a step closer to her. Confidence radiated from her in the tilt of her chin, the arch of her eyebrows, the heated look in her eyes. She set her belongings on the hood of a nearby car.

Slowly, she moved to stand so close to him that the heat of her body touched him and her full lips beckoned, a breath from his. "And now it's that time again."

He gave in to the urge to lean in and inhale the sweet scent of her. "Time for what?"

The corner of her mouth tilted in a slight smile. "Time for me to take a new lover, of course."

4

A GULL SWOOPED LOW overhead, a reminder of their proximity to the beach. A salt-tinged breeze stirred the humid air.

Tess's heart pounded. If ever a man needed healing, Mason Davies did. He seemed so calm and collected on the outside, but inside…inside he was a mass of repressed emotions. If her aunt Sophie was right and most illness originated in what she called the emotional body, then his condition would likely deteriorate if he continued to deny himself.

Right now, the man's emotions bubbled in turmoil. He wanted Tess, but he fought it. If she was going to help him, she had to work fast. As she faced him, her healing alarm clanged a red alert.

She held her breath as Mason's brown eyes rounded. Desire flowed off him and she smiled to herself, confidence filling her. She could help this man. What a lovely new companion he'd make.

He brushed a lock of hair from her cheek. "Are you always this bold?"

"I don't like games. I believe in laying all my cards on the table." She cocked her head. "I want you. You want me. Sounds pretty straightforward."

"Nothing's that straightforward these days."

"Sure it is. With me, what you see is what you get."

"Do *you* always get what you want?"

"Not always, but a lot of the time."

"And you want me?"

She snuggled in closer and dropped her arms around his neck. "Oh, yes."

"You think I want you?"

"I don't think, I know."

"You're awfully confident."

"Let's just say that I have a knack for sensing these things."

He nodded toward the restaurant. "And all of those men in there and the ones calling on your cell phone... they want you, too?"

"Oh, no. Maybe once, but not so much anymore."

"Not so much?"

"No."

He shook his head in obvious disbelief. "Right, that's why they're all calling and hanging around."

"A lot of that was coincidence."

"For that much coincidence you have to have a lot of men hanging around."

"I have my fair share...maybe a little more. But they do move on eventually."

"They move on, or *you* move on?"

"Both. Does it matter?"

His features darkened. "It does to me."

"You want to be the one moving on."

"It's preferable, don't you think? No one likes being left behind."

"Why does someone have to be left behind? Why can't you both move on?"

"That's just not realistic. In the real world people get left behind. End of story."

So, Mason *did* have abandonment issues.

How ironic that she, of all people, would be so drawn to him. Not that she'd ever abandoned anyone, but she'd seen more than her share of goodbyes. "It doesn't have to be that way."

"Right." He glanced away. "Whatever you say."

"Mason." She waited until his eyes again met hers. "Come out with me, right now. We'll spend a quiet afternoon, just the two of us. We'll talk, get to know each other—see what comes of it."

His gaze traveled down to her breasts, then back up to her face. "Maybe we shouldn't…you know, now that we're working together."

"I think getting to know each other better can only enhance our working relationship."

"Really?"

"Most definitely."

He inhaled a deep breath. "And what would we do— just the two of us?"

"Whatever we want to."

A short laugh escaped him. "Yeah, that's what I'm afraid of."

Smiling, she pushed away from him. "We're on, then. It's a date."

"Wait, not so fast."

She paused, frowning at the determination in his eyes. But he wanted her. Would he really deny himself—deny them both? "Come on, Mason. It'll be fun."

"I have to check on a couple of patients at the hospital this afternoon." As if to reinforce his responsibilities, his cell phone chimed. He dug it out of his pocket, checking the number on the display.

He turned to her, his eyes apologetic. "I have to take this. Hold on." He moved a short distance away and spoke in quiet tones for a few moments before returning to her. "I'm sorry. I have to go."

"Right." Disappointment swirled through her. So, this was what rejection felt like. Go figure. "We can get together another time."

His smile brightened his entire face. "How about tomorrow night?"

She nearly bounced with joy. "Saturday? That would be great. You want to meet somewhere? I know this really funky club—"

"I'll pick you up at seven."

"Oh, okay."

"I'll take you to dinner, maybe the theater. I'll show you that sometimes the old tried and true is the best way to have a good time."

Pride glimmered off him. The man had to be in control. He had to do things his way.

That was all fine for now. Later, once he had gotten comfortable with her, she would shake him up a little—ease him into some fun on the lighter side. Every nerve in her being told her it was of the utmost importance that she help Mason break out of his conventional ways and learn to be spontaneous. But evidently she needed to gain his confidence first.

"Okay, Mason. We'll do it your way this time, but

you have to promise me that the next time we do it all my way. I call the shots."

"I love your confidence. You're sure there'll be a next time?"

"Oh, yeah." Her blood warmed as she thought of all the good times headed their way. "Tomorrow night is just the beginning, love, make no mistake about that."

PIANO MUSIC FLOATED from the open lounge area above the restaurant where Mason sat across from Tess. Wide windows displayed a clear view of the intercoastal, lit by the lights of a nearby pier and the numerous boats traversing the evening waters.

He relaxed in his chair as she took a tentative sip of her wine, smiling her pleasure at the robust flavor. She was stunning tonight. Not that she'd looked bad on any of their previous encounters, but tonight she seemed almost radiant.

"That's a beautiful dress." He nodded toward the slinky black number she wore, wishing he knew better words to describe exactly how lovely she looked. The dress accentuated her curves, making them impossible to ignore. His pulse thrummed.

"Thanks. You clean up nice yourself."

Their server approached, dwarfed by the huge dishes she carried. Her eyes sparkled as she set their entrées before them. "Here you go, Dr. Davies, the snapper with snow peas and new potatoes, just the way you like them, light on the salt and butter."

"You're spoiling me, Donna." Mason grinned at the woman. This was what he liked—a restaurant where they knew him and his preferences.

"You're one of our best customers and we aim to please."

He surveyed the steaming dishes on the table. "You've certainly done that. Everything look okay to you, Tess?"

Tess breathed in the aroma of her steak and loaded baked potato. "It smells heavenly." She took a taste of the potato and closed her eyes as she savored the bite. "Delicious. Could we get some more rolls, please?"

"Yes, ma'am, I'll bring them right over."

"And butter?" Tess asked.

"Certainly." Donna turned to Mason. "Anything else for you, Doctor? More wine?"

"No, I'm fine, thanks."

The woman nodded, then hurried away, weaving a path through the white-covered tables. Tess cut into her steak and he took a bite of his fish. "You want to try some?" he asked her. "The chef here is wonderful."

She leaned toward him. "You really like this place, don't you?"

"Andre's is the best. Been coming here for years."

"It's all wonderful as far as I can see. Great food and service. Nice atmosphere."

"What else could you ask for in a restaurant?"

"Nothing. It's perfect."

Warmth filled him. Her approval pleased him more than he wanted to admit. "Exactly."

"Except…"

"What?" He stopped with his fork halfway to his mouth. "You just said it was perfect."

Her gaze pinned him. "Define 'best customer.'"

He stared at her, frowning. "What do you mean? I'm

a regular customer. I'm friendly and appreciative. I take care of the staff."

"Define 'regular.'"

What was she getting at? "Regular. I dine here often."

"How often?"

"What's with all the questions?"

She shrugged. "I have this feeling about you, Mason."

Something told him this wasn't the kind of feeling he was going to like. "What kind of feeling?"

Her lips pursed. "You like the tried and true."

"That's right."

"You like being where you're known and where you know people."

"Who doesn't?"

"You like knowing what to expect and what's expected of you."

He raised his hands in appeal. "Is that a bad thing?"

"Ever feel like you're in a rut?"

"No." A rut? Who was in a rut?

"You don't ever find yourself doing the same thing over and over again?"

"I like a routine. What's wrong with that?"

"Define 'routine.'"

"Come on, Tess, what are you driving at?" He swallowed. How could the woman badger him and still look so damn tempting?

"I don't know you well enough to make any judgments, but there's a fine line between a routine and a rut."

"Well, I am not in a rut. I eat here three, maybe four times a week, because I like it for all the reasons we've already stated. That does not mean I'm in a rut. I'm happy with my life. People in ruts are not happy with their lives." He took a sip of his wine to calm himself.

The woman had a way of riling him.

"No need to get all defensive. You do agree that a little change is healthy, right?"

He stiffened. "Change is part of life. I accept that. I can roll with the punches as well as the next guy."

"But change can be a good thing. It isn't always about rolling with the punches. Sometimes it's about going with the flow. Ever do that? Jump in a raft and let the current take you?"

"Some of us don't have the time or inclination to just drift about."

"You should try it sometime." She ran her finger along the edge of her wineglass. "Imagine the two of us, drifting along together with the sun warming us, a nice breeze caressing our skin." Her gaze met his, the blue of her eyes as enticing as ever. "No phones or pagers. Just all the time in the world to enjoy each other."

His mouth ran dry as she took a long swallow of wine. Visions of her floating along in the water wearing nothing but sunshine filled his head. "Well, honey, when you put it that way, it does have a certain appeal."

"Of course it does. You know I'd take really good care of you."

"I have no doubt you would."

Her smile—filled with promise for the night to come—sent heat rippling through him. He smiled back at her, ignoring all the warning bells going off in his head. He could enjoy a night with her and not get tied up in a relationship.

As far as he could tell, Tess didn't have relationships. She had affairs, which were by nature temporary. "I suppose drifting might not be a bad thing as long as one knew in advance that it would be a short trip."

"The point of·drifting is that you land where and when you land, with no predetermined time frame. But since it's new to you, I'd say a short bout—a testing of the waters—would be in order."

He raised his glass, letting his gaze fall briefly to the swell of her breasts. "To a testing of the waters."

She clinked her glass to his. "May it be all we've dreamed and more." She held his gaze while they both drank deeply.

Notes from the piano shifted into a livelier tune. Tess took another bite of her food, while he continued sipping his wine. The murmur of voices filled the space around them, but their booth remained a private refuge amid the bustle of the restaurant.

"So, tell me about your family. Parents, siblings?" she asked.

"I have a few uncles." He set down his glass and picked up his fork, clenching it in his fist.

"Uncles?"

"Yes, uncles. That's it. No parents. No siblings."

She blinked. "Oh, Mason, I'm so sorry."

When she reached for his hand, he pulled back. This one with her questions. She'd probably keep asking until she told her. "The quick of it is that my mother split when I was a kid and my father drank himself to death shortly after. I was passed from uncle to uncle until I could make it on my own. End of story. End of discussion. So how about you?"

She sat straighter, but seemed to take his brusque explanation in stride, nodding almost as if she'd expected as much. "Let's see, I have a mother who's usually off traveling somewhere, two sisters, both of whom I lived with until one moved out recently. I'm pretty sure the other one is still there, though I don't see much of her these days. I also have an aunt, my mother's sister, who's around most of the time and who keeps us all sane. And we have a family friend who's more like a father to us than anything, though he's not a blood relation."

"Sounds like quite a crew." He set down his fork and pushed away his plate. In spite of himself, envy ate at him. Her tone was warm as she spoke of her family.

He mentally shook himself. No use wishing for something he wasn't meant to have. He had his uncles. They were family enough.

"What are your uncles like?"

"They're okay." He shrugged. "Stout Republicans, doctors mostly, old school. My favorite is Uncle Gabe. He's my mother's brother. I lived with him the longest. I don't really have anything to do with them these days, though." He glanced at his watch. "We should get going if we don't want to be late."

"Late?"

He smiled, again on stable ground. "Yes, my dear, the theater awaits us."

MUSIC SWELLED IN THE darkened theater. The audience sat seemingly entranced as the actors moved across the stage at the Coconut Grove Playhouse. Tess stretched and glanced surreptitiously at her watch.

How much longer could this play last?

Not that she wasn't enjoying it. As far as plays went,

this one wasn't bad. She was just finding sitting still for such a long time a bit challenging. Mason appeared to be into the drama and his pleasure was always nice to feel.

It made her think of a different kind of pleasure, though, and she was itching to get the man alone. He, however, seemed in no hurry to leave. It was disconcerting to have him so oblivious to her.

Did he not realize what a true hunk he was?

She shifted in her seat. A man of convention. Good God, what if he didn't believe in kissing on the first date?

He glanced at her and smiled, his attention diverted from the play long enough to squeeze her hand and let his gaze drift over her. She'd chosen this dress with seduction in mind and he hadn't been unaffected by it throughout the evening. His focus lingered over her breasts, her cleavage exposed just enough to tantalize.

She leaned toward him, so her leg pressed into his. She lowered her hand to her thigh and slipped from his grasp, so his hand rested on her, warming her through the thin fabric of her dress. His fingers flexed over her and desire buzzed around them.

Smiling, she slid her hand up his chest and raised her face to him. His gaze fastened on her mouth. He cupped her cheek, then leaned in close to whisper in her ear, "Don't be a tease, Tess. I promise to kiss you later."

"Later?" Sighing, she rubbed her cheek against his, her lips a breath from his. "Why not now?"

He groaned softly and frustration sounded in his voice. "This isn't the proper place or time."

"Who wants to be proper? It's dark and no one's paying any attention to us."

She skimmed her mouth along his jaw, then brushed

his lips with hers. He stilled for a long moment as heat spiraled out from him. She absorbed his desire, darting her tongue along his full bottom lip.

He pulled away, his muscles rigid. "Not here."

She pressed her hand over his, where he gripped her thigh. If he thought she'd give up so easily when he obviously wanted her, he was sorely mistaken. The man was way too into this repression and she could sense the toll it had already taken. Before all was through, she'd show him the wonders of embracing his desires.

Slowly, his hand relaxed as he made a pretense of watching the play. She stroked his long fingers until the tension in him lessened. She shifted, so his hand slipped farther up her leg. Pausing, she drank in his heightened awareness, almost feeling the thudding of his heart. His fingers flexed again, then tightened. She prepared for him to pull away, but instead, he made an exploratory circle with his thumb.

Taking a deep breath, she savored the moment where he hovered on the verge of giving in, but the action on the stage picked up and the audience burst into a round of spontaneous applause. Mason clapped along with them, leaving the impression of his hand burning on her thigh.

For a moment she was disappointed, but as soon as the applause died, he seized her hand and rose. She grabbed her purse and followed as he maneuvered to the aisle, then out the door.

"What? We're leaving? And before the end of that most engrossing play?" she asked, all innocence when they reached the lobby.

"That's right and don't you dare complain. You asked for this."

"I did?" she asked as he towed her out onto the street.

He didn't spare her a glance as he made a beeline for the car. "Indeed you did."

"But where are we going?"

As he yanked open the door for her, he gave her a fierce frown. She had a flash of him as a warrior of old, dealing with his latest conquest. Her pulse quickened.

"I'm taking you home, where I am going to kiss you," he said.

Smiling, she brushed up against him. "Then…?"

The ghost of a smile floated across his lips. "Then you get what you want."

She cocked her head. "And what do I want?"

His gaze pierced her. "Me."

5

TESS EYED MASON AS HE ushered her into his compact kitchen. The chrome surfaces and neat cabinets spoke of efficiency. A digital clock on the wall showed that it was just after eleven. She turned to him smiling. "So…"

He scooped her against him with one arm as he lowered his mouth to hers. He stopped, a breath away. "Now for that kiss."

She shivered, both from the cold of the air-conditioned house and in anticipation. His lips brushed hers, caressing her with deepening strokes, until she opened to let him explore at his leisure. As promised, he took his time. He tasted of mint and an excitement that she hadn't expected in him. Below all his careful reserve, Mason Davies was a man full of surprises.

His tongue soothed hers with slow, steady strokes, kindling her desire and sending her blood thrumming. She'd known she'd enjoy kissing him. She pressed her body closer to his and shivered again.

"Cold?" He broke away to rub his hands up and down her arms.

"Excited."

"Really?"

"Kiss me again and see for yourself."

"Yes, ma'am."

He lowered his mouth to hers once more, but this time his tongue was more demanding, his hands bolder in their exploration as he swept them down her back to cup her bottom. She wrapped her arms around his neck and pressed her body close to his. His pleasure—his excitement—radiated to her, mingling with the rampant emotions rushing through her. It had never felt like this.

And this was just a kiss.

His hands slipped down to the hemline of her dress, then underneath to her skin. Every nerve in her body came alive as he skimmed his fingers up the back of her thighs to her buttocks, bared by the thong she wore. He kissed her again while kneading her, until she whimpered and hooked her leg around his in an effort to move closer.

When one of his hands found her breast she sighed with delight. He maneuvered past her bra, until the warmth of his fingers melted into her. Her nipple beaded under his careful ministrations, sending tendrils of wicked desire licking through her.

Her fingers fumbled on his shirt buttons before she could run her hand along his firm abs and chest. He stalled in his attentions for a moment as she found his nipples and plucked them to attention. Then he was on her in full force, lifting her to the counter and nestling himself between her legs. Her dress loosened, then slipped down to her waist as he kissed her and seemed to touch her everywhere at once. She lost herself in the sensations, the building heat.

Cool air from a vent above them hit her as he slipped off her bra, but first his breath, then his mouth warmed her. He sucked hard on her breast, taking her nipple into his mouth and teasing the tip with his tongue, until she closed her eyes and moaned.

"Oh, Mason, that feels so good."

She stroked his hair, surprised at its softness, then gasped as his fingers found the folds of her femininity. Without prelude he thrust deep, but she was wet and eager for his attentions. His thumb caressed her clit, while he drove two fingers into her. Never breaking his rhythm, he nibbled his way to her other breast where he laved her to the brink of endurance.

"Oh…sweet…"

He answered with a sound of pleasure from deep in his throat and she lost all thought as he increased his pace. With true magic in his touch he pleasured her, until the sexual tension coiling inside her built to an unbearable pitch. Meeting him thrust for thrust, she gripped his shoulders as the first tremors of orgasm hit her. Her body tightened as blinding white bliss burst through her and she cried out, the sound tearing from her throat.

She melted against him, too drained to even hold on properly when he carried her into his bedroom. He turned on the light and desire shone in his eyes as he deposited her on the bed. She lay limp as he stripped off her disheveled clothes, then slowly removed his own, his gaze never leaving her.

She licked dry lips at the sight of him. He was as magnificent a man as she had ever seen. His build was adequate, but he had that bearing of the warrior she had glimpsed earlier. And his evident desire was a force to be reckoned with. A sigh left her at the thought of all the pleasure he was so well equipped to deliver.

She managed a weak smile, her muscles still feeling a little like jelly. When had she ever been this spent after just one orgasm? And he hadn't even been inside her yet. How would she feel after that? "Do with me as you will. I am too drained to protest. Besides, I kind of like the thought of you losing control."

His lips thinned and a cloud seemed to pass over his features. As she'd suspected, she'd hit on another sore spot. She opened her arms to him. "We'll take it any way you want it, Mason."

He moved to the bed and covered her with his body, bracing himself on his elbows. When he kissed her, she slipped her hand down to caress his erection. Ah, the feel of him—so vibrant, so very alive. She stroked him until he nuzzled her ear.

"I want to be inside you," he murmured, his voice low and gruff.

"I want you inside me."

His gaze met hers and, for a moment, she felt exposed, as though he could see into her soul. Then he moved away to ready himself. After he'd rolled on a condom he returned to her, his body hot and wonderfully hard. She let him arrange her like a rag doll, happy to have him take control as he draped her legs over his shoulders.

It was strange, really, this lethargy. Normally she was full of energy and well in charge of her sexual encounters. How nice it was to let him lead for a change. They both watched him slip slowly into her, intent on the joining of their bodies. She shifted as he eased his way in, giving her time to adjust to him.

Goodness, the man was big.

When he was fully seated, he raised his head and his gaze found hers. For a long moment, he didn't move as he seemed to search for something in her eyes—acceptance? Warmth filled her and she embraced him, squeezing him tight with her inner muscles, encouraging him to let loose some of the immense control he possessed.

At long last he exhaled, his breath brushing her face as he moved. Her body came alive with each deliberate thrust, her nerve endings tingling. He touched her clit while he loved her, stroking in and out with a grace that matched his strength.

She shuddered as the tension again coiled within her, each thrust bringing her closer to that pinnacle, the magic of his fingers again on her surpassed only by the power of his loving. This warrior knew how to wield his sword.

As he stroked her into a fit of arousal a strange euphoria filled her. Each thrust brought her closer to the realization that she was head over heels infatuated with him.

"Oh...hell...Tess." The muscles in his neck bunched as he strained to keep his steady pace.

She rocked against him, so caught up in the sensations stirring her, she could barely speak. "It's okay... just...let...go."

A shudder passed through him and he closed his eyes. His mouth opened in a wordless cry as he plunged into her, yet his movements never varied from his rhythm, in spite of the need racking his body. He gripped her bottom and thrust hard and long, rising to his knees, so she was spread before him on the bed. She gripped a fistful of blanket and arched into him as waves of desire washed over her. His movements became frenzied, though he clenched his jaw with restraint.

She gasped as she rode with him to a place of indescribable pleasure. Her clit burned and her sex throbbed as her blood pounded through her. Heat rippled outward from her core. He thrust deep, deeper, her muscles clenching him as the first spasm of orgasm hit her. She cried out, caught up in a world-shattering release that left her weightless and floating, barely aware as Mason yelled and emptied himself deep inside her.

If she'd been limp before, she was positively wilted now. He lifted her and held her close to him. How he had the strength not to collapse beside her she could hardly fathom. She draped her arms around his neck and nestled against him, letting him support her, her blood pounding where their bodies remained joined.

For a while he seemed content to cradle her against him, while his breath rasped near her ear. Someone's heartbeat thudded, the pulse steady and strong—whether it was his or hers, she couldn't tell, so entwined they seemed at that moment.

When his breathing slowed he placed first one kiss, then another along her neck. Soon he feasted passionately on an area she had never thought to be quite so arousing, until now. She smiled and rolled her head to the side to give him better access.

"Tess…" He seemed to savor her name and a delicious warmth spread again through her. "Tess, you are so lovely. Most tasty."

She cupped his cheek and brought his mouth to hers,

suddenly hungry for his kiss. Where *she* got the energy was another mystery, but he energized her in a way she wouldn't have thought possible a moment ago. He seemed to buzz with renewed vitality.

"What a woman." He placed a particularly loud smack on her shoulder.

She laughed. "Well, *you're* the man."

His chest puffed out with pride. "Yeah, I *am* the man."

Giggles bubbled out of her. She felt good. "Absolutely."

He joined her and it seemed their laughter lifted them up, until he pressed his face against hers, his beautiful mouth spread into a wide smile. "I don't think I've ever felt this...I don't know, free."

She nuzzled her nose against his. "It only gets better from here."

Tilting his head, he covered her mouth with his. His kiss began teasing and light, but soon heated, his tongue stroking hers with an increasing hunger. He caressed her breasts and flicked her nipples with his thumbs. Passion flamed again through her, and an answering wave rose from him as she ground against him.

His cock stirred inside her. Her heart quickened and she moved her hips, savoring the exquisite feel of her clit rubbing him, while he again filled her, stretching her to her limit. Their recent encounter seemed to have done nothing to lessen his virility.

He broke the kiss to stare at her in wonder. "Look what you're doing to me. I can't seem to get enough of you. What kind of woman are you that you can arouse a man so quickly after draining him?"

"Right now I'd say I'm an insatiable one, and, like I said, I always get what I want."

She'd had this reaction from men before, but it was her own answering hunger that surprised her. She had been uncustomarily sapped just moments before. That he could stir this intense response in her again so quickly was somehow significant.

With Mason it seemed she wasn't completely in control. She delved her fingers into his hair and rocked against him, eliciting a sharp intake of breath on his part as he gripped her hips and settled once more into a steady rhythm with her.

THE SOUND OF A CHIME filtered to Mason through a sleep-filled haze. He came awake slowly, increasingly aware of the warm weight pressed to his side. Smiling, he turned to slide his arm around…Tess.

He opened one eye. A tangle of fiery waves cascaded over his shoulder. Brushing the heavy mass aside, he peered at the beauty in his bed. Their evening together had proved that he was powerless to resist her, even in the face of his strict upbringing.

Images of his night with her drifted through his mind: her nipples pink and wet with his loving; his erection slipping inside her; the look of bliss on her face as she drifted to sleep in his arms. His mouth watered with the memory of her taste, his fingers itched for the feel of her soft skin, and his cock stirred in anticipation of slipping inside her again.

Who was in a rut now?

It was unbelievable enough that he'd been able to love her throughout the night, but damned if the woman could get him all riled up and she wasn't even awake yet. He should be sacked out, recuperating from the workout she'd given him. He closed his eyes and tried to count the number of times he had taken her during the night, but his mind hazed in a fog of lust.

And here he was as hard as a freaking rock, ready to go at it again. She had turned him into some kind of sex-crazed maniac. Still, a man shouldn't look a gift horse in the mouth. Whatever well this new sexual energy came from, it made no sense to waste it.

He reached under the sheet to cup her breast. Circling his thumb, he coaxed her nipple into a hard point. She moaned softly and stretched, shifting in her sleep, unconsciously giving him better access.

The sheet slipped, revealing the pink tip, and he couldn't resist lowering his mouth over her. He suckled her, savoring the sexy sounds she made and the fumbling of her hands over him as she came awake. She stroked her fingers down his chest, warming his blood. She plucked at his nipples, sending tendrils of heat curling through him.

"Good morning, Mason." Her voice was low and throaty and sexy as hell. She stretched again and made a soft sighing sound that made him groan in response.

"Mmm, that's so nice. You have such a talented mouth," she said.

In answer he kissed a path to her other breast, circling her nipple with the point of his tongue, until she arched and reached for his aching cock.

He closed his eyes as her fingers clasped him, and she stroked him with just the right pressure. He shifted up beside her. "How can I want you again like this?"

A smile pulled at her lips. "It's a gift."

He inhaled sharply as she squeezed the delicate head.

All his nerve endings came alert and warmth spread out from his belly. He groaned as she moved over him, her hair fanning across his stomach and thighs as she maneuvered lower to where her hand still worked him. When her mouth closed over him it was all he could do to hold on and endure the exquisite pleasure.

No woman had ever given to him the way Tess gave to him at that moment. She took her time, laving his entire length, feasting on the head, then sucking him into her hot mouth, until he groaned and bucked beneath her, near the brink of his control.

"Tess," he ground out through gritted teeth. "I can't take any more."

With one last pull of her mouth, she moved up his body, then kissed him, her tongue demanding. She straddled him, nestling her sex against his, so he had to fist his hands again to keep from moving and slipping inside her unprotected.

At last she broke the kiss, and the desire in her eyes would have brought him to his knees had he been standing. She reached for a condom on the nightstand, but he stopped her. "Not so fast. I haven't had my breakfast."

Her eyebrows arched. "You're hungry?"

"Starved, it seems." He let his gaze drift to her pubic hair.

She bit her bottom lip and relaxed on the pillow. "Well, I wouldn't want to be anything less than accommodating."

"No, that wouldn't do."

She spread her knees to make room for him and he moved between her legs, the scent of her arousal stirring him. He took his time savoring the sight of her luscious flesh, already swollen and wet. He touched her first, caressing her, parting her to reveal her hidden treasure, before he lowered his mouth.

No morning feast had ever tasted sweeter. The soft sighs Tess uttered sent his blood pounding through his veins. He licked her folds before centering on her clit. Her fingers threaded through his hair and she tilted her pelvis to him. Soon she shuddered and stiffened beneath him, her moan of pleasure curling around him.

He reached out and grabbed the condom. Heavy lidded, she watched him as he rolled it on. When he moved over her she kissed him quickly, then pulled back.

"Wait," she said, then turned onto her stomach. "Like this."

Her bottom nestled against his erection and he wasted no time in lifting her up and planting himself inside her. The long night must have finally taken its toll. He came almost immediately, then collapsed on top of her.

"That's it," he murmured in her ear. "You've finally worn me out."

She rose up on one elbow and frowned at him. "That's too bad."

"Don't be disappointed. I'll get my strength back. Just let me rest a little bit, then I'll be ready to go."

"Great, it's a date."

"A date? Is that what you call it?" He waggled his eyebrows at her.

"I am not talking about sex...though there *will* be more of that later. I'm actually a little oversated myself."

A sense of uncertainty gripped him. "Then what are you talking about?"

"It's Sunday and you're off, right?"

His stomach tightened. "Well, I'm always on call, but yes, I'm off for the day."

"Then it's my turn."

"Your turn?"

"Don't act like you don't remember. I agreed to go out with you last night on your terms. I ate dinner at that restaurant with you, then sat through that play."

"You liked the restaurant."

"Don't avoid the point here."

He rolled to his back, the knot in his stomach turning into a feeling of impending doom. "And that point is?"

She leaned over him, a wicked gleam dancing in her eyes. "Today is my pick. Today we share a completely spontaneous and *fun* day."

"Spontaneous?"

"And fun. We're going to drift."

"You mean what we were doing last night—and just now—wasn't drifting?"

"I suppose that was drifting of one sort."

"There's another?"

She nodded.

He hesitated a long moment, fighting the unease that had gripped him. Okay, so maybe he had envisioned spending the entire day in bed with her, but this didn't sound so bad. Spontaneous and fun didn't necessarily spell disaster. He squelched the warning alarms in his head and sat up, lifting his chin high.

He could do this. He could meet this challenge. A single day of spontaneity couldn't derail a lifetime of discipline. "I'm yours then—for the day."

"You said it, mister." She grabbed his hand and before he changed his mind tugged him out of the bed and toward the bathroom. "You're mine."

He perked up. "Are we taking a shower together?"

"A quick one." She turned and frowned at him. "Just a shower—no sex. We don't have time for that. The sun is up and time's wasting."

Disappointment mingled with his returning dread. "Wouldn't want to *waste* any time."

"Don't look so glum. We'll get back to that. I promise. But there's a whole world to explore and good times to be had. We're getting you out of your rut and into the new and exciting."

"But we did that last night. If that wasn't new and exciting, I don't know what is."

She smiled at him. "Yes, it was. It was a good start, but this isn't just about sex. You'll feel better for it. You'll see."

"Right." He padded along behind her. Good times. Something told him they had very different ideas of what constituted a good time.

6

MASON STARED AT THE brightly painted building near the beach. "You're kidding. There is absolutely no way I am going in there."

"Come on. You can't tell me you've never been to an arcade."

He never had, but he wasn't going to admit that to her. "Arcades are for kids."

"No, they're not."

"Yes—" he nodded to some children pushing through the door "—they are."

"Well, even *you* must have been a kid at one time."

"Nope, never."

She grabbed his hand and pulled him into the dimly lit interior. Multicolored lights flashed from various games lining the walls and grouped about the open center area. Various dings, tones and computerized notes sounded from all corners.

He wrinkled his nose at the sour smell that permeated the air, while eyeing the blotchy carpet in distrust. "I don't know about this."

"Oh, come on. It isn't going to hurt you to have a little fun."

"I have fun."

She folded her arms and gave him a wide-eyed look, waiting for him to elaborate.

"You know, like last night. I go out to dinner and the theater on occasion."

"That was really nice, Mason, but I mean *Fun* with a capital *F.*"

He scratched his head. "I'm taking Rafe to a game next Saturday."

"Good, but my guess is that's more for Project Mentor and Rafe. I'm talking about fun for you, where you let go of your inhibitions and enjoy yourself, regardless of what anyone else might think. Fun outside the bedroom. Last night was about us. This is about fun for you. Just for you. When was the last time you did something just because it was something *you* wanted to do? Something besides sex."

When *was* the last time he'd had that kind of fun? "I like football and lacrosse."

"Playing it or watching it?"

"I haven't done much more than watch it in years, but I used to play."

"Doesn't count." She grabbed his hand again and pulled him toward a low counter at one end of the building.

While she purchased what she called a game card, he eyed a row of plastic rings and other unidentifiable, but seemingly just as useless, objects proudly displayed beneath the grimy glass countertop. "And exactly what would you do with any of that?"

She flashed him a grin and nodded toward a row of stuffed animals lining a shelf on the wall behind the counter. "I don't go for the small stuff."

"I see. I didn't realize I was with a big winner."

"This way."

She maneuvered her way past a guy on a pair of skis, poling his way down a snowy terrain depicted on a screen in front of him, a circular table with spinning lights and buttons that did who knew what and an air-hockey table. At least that Mason recognized. A loud banging sounded from around a corner. Tess swerved toward the sound, stopping beside a small girl who viciously hammered mechanical rodents as they popped out of an assortment of holes.

"I love this one." Tess's face glowed with excitement.

"Hammering rodents?" He leaned back as the girl made a particularly wild swing.

"They're gophers." Tess rolled her eyes at him as though he should have been able to recognize the creatures before they disappeared.

"Of course, gophers. What else?"

The game played out and the young girl squealed when the machine spit out a string of tickets. Tess took her place as the youngster ran off toward the prize counter.

"So, the more rodents you hit, the more prize tickets you get?"

Tess fed her card into the machine, then raised the hammer. "You catch on quick."

The music wound out and she swung her hammer with a vengeance, hardly missing the little guys as they popped up. Mason folded his arms and let his gaze drift over her as she focused on the game, her expression stern with concentration. What was it about this woman that attracted him?

Her nose sloped a little long. Her lips were almost

too full, but somehow put all together, her features worked. She flashed him a triumphant glance and he nodded to himself. It was her eyes. Tess had the most amazing blue eyes he'd ever seen.

And the woman could swing a hammer. He winced as she struck a mechanical gopher and laughed. The sound curled around him rich and full, drawing his own laugh from him.

"Okay, your turn." She held the large rubber hammer out to him.

He backed away, his hands raised to ward her off. "No, thanks."

"It's a great way to get out all your aggressions."

"I don't have any aggressions."

"Sure you do. Everyone does."

"Nope." He folded his arms across his chest and planted his feet wide. "I keep a rational head."

"That's what concerns me. I say you're suppressing your emotions."

"What? No. I express my emotions just fine, thank you very much. I laughed with you, didn't I? I was having a good time."

"You were living vicariously. Until you're doing the actual hammering you haven't really experienced the art of gopher bashing."

"I'll pass."

The familiar sound of her cell phone mingled with the clatter of the game room. She pulled her phone from her purse to check the number, then put it back without answering.

Something about her ease in shrugging off the caller irritated him. Was it another one of her former lovers?

How long would it be before she stopped taking Mason's calls?

She stared at him a long moment, before shaking her head. "I'm afraid that our work here is done."

"What work? What do you mean?""

"Our work in transforming you."

"Transforming me?"

"Yep, I misjudged. You're not quite ready for this. It's time for plan B."

"Plan B?" He pursed his lips. "You mean more spontaneity."

"That's right." Her eyes sparkled with mischief. "Follow me. I'm hot. Let's cool off."

Once more she grabbed his hand. This time she led him out of the cool arcade into the blinding sunlight. He blinked to allow his eyes to adjust.

"Hear that?" She cocked her head.

He frowned as a gull screeched overhead and the dull roar of the surf floated over a row of colorful shops. She motioned for him to follow, then struck off toward the sound. He trailed in her wake.

What had he gotten into?

"THE BEACH?" MASON GLANCED from his leather shoes to where Tess stood knee deep and laughing in the foamy spray. She'd taken off her shoes and had her skirt tied up faster than he could catch his breath. "We're not exactly dressed for the beach."

"It feels wonderful." She squealed as a wave splashed over her. "Come in."

"I think I might have preferred the gopher bashing. Maybe I'll just watch you for a bit."

"That's no fun." She splashed water in his direction, inadvertently soaking her top so the thin fabric clung to her breasts.

"Don't be so sure."

A devilish light shone in her eyes. She splashed again, liberally wetting herself, this time apparently on purpose. "I had better warn you. This is *not* a spectator sport."

"I don't know. Looks pretty good to me." He settled on his haunches. A gull swooped overhead as a bead of sweat rolled down his temple. It was the first week of October. How could it still be so blasted hot?

She ran her hand across her belly. "Don't be so sure. *Feels* even better."

The whir of a Jet Ski floated over the breeze. Laughter rose from a cluster of people farther along the beach. The sun beat down on Mason and sparkled off the water all around Tess. He swallowed, his leg muscles cramping. Trailing his fingers in the white sand, he kept his gaze on Tess as she played in the surf.

"Come on in, Mason." She gestured to him, her eyes beseeching.

He shifted to sit in the sand, his throat dry. Maybe he could take his shoes off, cool his feet a little. He removed his loafers and nearly sighed in relief as the air hit his feet.

"Dip your toes in." Her smile enticed him. "It's just water. Nothing to be afraid of."

"It isn't the water that worries me."

Still he rolled up his pants, then rose and walked gingerly over the sand, wincing as bits of crushed shell bit into his feet. He stepped into the water, just beyond the shore where the waves ebbed and flowed in a lulling motion.

"Ah…" The water lapped around his ankles, bathing his feet in refreshing coolness. He wiggled his toes as Tess sloshed toward him.

"See, you should always listen to me. I know what feels good." She sidled up beside him, her wet skin glistening in the late afternoon sun.

"I have no doubts about that." He leaned away from her. "You're soaked."

"It's a heavenly release from this humidity."

He glanced down at his not-so-crisp shirt. The afternoon had taken a toll on his clothes. Never had he sported more wrinkles.

Laughing, Tess turned, then dove into the deeper water, submerging for several long strokes. Mason shook his head. The woman meant to wreak havoc with a lifetime of precise conditioning.

If his uncles could see him now…

He stared longingly after her as she floated on her back, a smile of pure satisfaction on her lips. Sweat rolled down his forehead. He stepped in farther. "Oh, the hell with it."

He dove after her. With blissful relief the surf closed over him. He pulled himself through the water with long strokes, coming up beside her as she treaded water.

She splashed him. "You're swimming in your clothes, Mason. There's hope for you yet."

He laughed. It felt good. Really good. When was the last time he'd laughed like this? A strange euphoria filled him. "Maybe you're not such a bad influence after all."

"Me? A bad influence?" She kicked closer to him, until the warmth of her body flowed over him. Her lips hovered just beneath his. "Never."

His gaze fastened on her mouth. He swayed closer

to her. Laughter from a group up the beach grew louder as some of the party moved in their direction.

"Maybe we should head out of here." He pushed away from her, toward the shore.

A seductive smile curved her lips. "But you were going to kiss me."

"Was I?"

"Yes, you were. I saw it in your eyes." She tilted her head in a familiar gesture. "What's wrong? Too stuffy to kiss me in public?"

"Just prefer some privacy. There's a time and place for everything. When I kiss you again, I intend to enjoy the hell out of it. Besides, kissing you tends to lead to other pursuits definitely not suited for public."

Her eyes widened as she followed him. "I'm sure there are certain ways we can be discreet in public."

He laughed and she frowned at him as she stepped from the water. "What's so funny?"

"You are many things, but I hardly see how you can be discreet. You're the kind of woman who draws every eye when she walks into a room."

Pink blossomed in her cheeks and she smiled. "Well, maybe just the men's." With a flick of her wet hair, she laughed and ran past him.

He stared after her, his enjoyment of the moment fading. Right, the men's. Tess was a man magnet and he was nothing more than her current lover. In a short time she would move on.

He would do well to remember that.

HUMMING SOFTLY THE following day, Tess set aside her watering can and fluffed her latest batch of gardenias.

Her aunt Sophie said no one could grow the temperamental flowers the way Tess could. She breathed deeply of the fragrant petals as memories of her weekend with Mason drifted through her mind: Mason resisting her at the theater; his hunger for her as he pleasured her in his kitchen; his immense control, even in the midst of their lovemaking.

The man was nothing short of magnificent, even as he resisted his innate need to cut loose.

"Where do you want these?" Victoria Green, Tess's new full-timer, lifted a crate of flowers.

"Those are for Mrs. Hammond. She won't be by until tomorrow to pick them up. Why don't you put them on the workbench in the back greenhouse? Make sure you note it under her customer profile, so we'll be able to find them when she comes."

"Customer profile is on the computer, right?"

"Yes. Tell you what, I need to enter the last shipment, so I'll take care of it." She headed for the small office she kept in the nursery's main building, but stopped and turned back. "I'm expecting my sister. Will you come get me when she arrives?

Victoria nodded, then strolled away carrying Mrs. Hammond's flowers. Tess sighed and glanced around the nursery, frowning. A sense of restlessness filled her. Everything was in order here at work and she had Mason now, who was a wonderful distraction. She'd been so happy with him over the weekend.

Life was good. So why this continuing feeling that there was some void in her life? She shrugged it off. The beach cleanup was this Saturday. Mason had said some of the teens would be there to help. Maybe she just needed some hands-on experience with Project Mentor to perk her up. Surely then she'd feel better about things.

She spent the next half hour catching up on the recent shipment and looking over the work schedule for the following week. She loved being able to take the weekend off. This was a relatively new luxury that she would enjoy all the more now that she had the good doctor to share it with.

Memories of her time with Mason brought a smile to her lips. The man was so unique. He was a puzzle she couldn't quite solve. For the most part he was all stern Mr. Rule-follower, but every now and then his resolve would slip, especially when they made love.

"Tess?" Victoria stood in the open door. "Your sister and a guy are here with a big truck."

"Thanks, Victoria."

Tess saved her work, before heading out to where Erin examined her latest assortment of trees. Thomas Scott, the man who was the closest thing to a father that the girls had ever known, stood by her side.

Erin glanced up and smiled, a sight Tess saw too little of these days. Maybe this was a sign that her little sister's mood had taken a turn for the better.

"I see you brought our number-one handyman." Tess grinned at Thomas.

"You get over here and give me a squeeze." He opened his arms to her and offered a smile of his own. "Why haven't I seen hide nor hair of you in ages? Your minions keeping you too busy?"

She laughed and hugged the man who had taught her to ride a bike without training wheels. "I've joined a women's group."

"You have?"

"I figured I needed to get involved again in a little charity work." She glanced at Erin. "That, and I've decided I can use a little less testosterone in my life."

"You can't be serious." Erin stared at her, one hand on her hip. "You're trading in your men for a women's group? That's hard to imagine. I can hardly move at the apartment without bumping into one of your men. Not that you've been around much lately."

Tess shrugged at her sister's look of censure. "I'm not tiring of anyone. As far as not being around I could say the same for you. I've been there. Just not over the weekend, but I called so you wouldn't worry."

"From the message you left you've found a new bauble for your collection."

"They are not a collection. They are individuals. Each is a wonderful man in his own right." And no one could ever categorize Mason along with the rest. He stood head and shoulders above all of her former lovers.

"Of course they are, sweetheart." Thomas looped an arm around each of them. He smiled at Tess. "Now, what have you got for your sister? Seems she's working on an entire duplex she needs greenery for. Should be a good piece of business for both of you."

"It is." Erin grinned, always content when involved in her work. "Did you get in the dracaenas we talked about?"

"Over here." Tess led her to a nearby grouping of the trees with their large decorative leaves. "I picked these four for you." She indicated the red sold tickets tied to the branches. "They're the healthiest."

"Oh, they're beautiful," Erin said as she fingered a leaf.

"Is it okay if I start loading them up, while you two work out the rest?" Thomas reached for a cart.

Tess slid the first tree closer to him. She glanced around for Evan, another one of her former lovers turned employee. "I've got a big hunky guy around here somewhere to help."

"Don't worry about it. I live to be of assistance to my girls."

"Okay, Thomas, but you have to promise to make me your famous apple pie soon, so we can catch up."

"Deal." He gave her a wink as he turned to his task of loading the trees.

An hour later she finished putting together the order for Erin. Her sister was great to do business with, knowledgeable and willing to work with her on a few special-order items.

Too bad their personal relationship never seemed to go as smoothly.

"So, you have a new guy." Erin turned to her as Thomas carted off the last of the load. They had filled the truck.

"Yes, his name is Mason Davies. He's a doctor."

"What kind?"

"He's an internist. He has a practice in Pembroke Pines. He has these dark eyes and the softest hair and a body that won't stop. The man is buff." Tess grinned with the thought of Mason's physique. "He helped found a free clinic in downtown Miami and this special organization, Project Mentor, that helps troubled kids—"

"Wow, you really like this guy."

"Well, yes, I do like him."

"You like him a lot. You're gushing over him. I've never seen you like this with any of your minions before. Look at you. You're positively beaming." Erin's voice was incredulous.

"I am not."

"Yes, you are. And he's a doctor. You haven't had one of those before, have you, except for that podiatrist a few years back?"

"Mason is a great guy. You'd like him."

"As long as he doesn't leave his dirty shorts lying around I'll love him. Are you bringing him by the apartment anytime soon?"

Tess paused. "I don't know. I haven't really thought about it. May have to clean house first."

"Do you mean you have to clean as in scrub the kitchen after Ramon has spent the afternoon whipping up his dish of the day?"

"Well, that, too."

A knowing light shone in her sister's eyes. "I see. You mean clean out your other minions."

Tess scowled. She was beginning to really dislike that word. "I just don't think he'd appreciate all the…disturbance the others tend to create."

"That's never been an issue with any of the others, has it?"

"No."

"So why worry about it now? Won't it work itself out?"

Why *was* she worrying about it? "I'm not sure. It just…wouldn't feel right to have him there with the others." She shrugged. "You're right. It's never been a problem before. It shouldn't matter now."

"But what you're saying is that this guy's special. That's great. I'm happy for you."

"Thanks."

A short silence fell over them, then Erin straightened. "Thomas is waiting."

She nodded toward where he sat smoking his pipe and regaling Evan, who'd finally shown up, with one of his stories. Thomas often had entertained the girls with wild stories of his youth. He'd filled a certain void in their lives.

Erin gestured to the clipboard Tess held. "Have you got everything you need to invoice me?"

Tess nodded. "I'll work in the discount we agreed on." She extended her hand. "Thanks."

"Yeah, no problem." Erin gave her a hardy shake. "Where else am I going to go for personal service and a great family discount?"

A feeling of heaviness descended on Tess as her sister walked away. Tess hadn't even asked Erin what she'd been up to lately. It seemed they never saw each other anymore, and when they did it was never quality time.

"Hey, Erin, wait up. I'll walk you out and say goodbye to Thomas." She ran to catch her sister.

They strode side by side toward Thomas and the truck. Tess glanced over at Erin. The two of them were so different. Erin was petite with smooth blond hair and green eyes. She favored her father, whom she'd actually met. Tess's father came from some far-off country their mother had visited in her earlier vagabond days. Tess wasn't sure if he even knew she existed or if Maggie had any idea how to reach him.

"So..." Tess broke the silence. "What's new with you?"

Erin shrugged. "Nothing, really. Been building up my business. I've been getting some really good bookings. Took a computer-design seminar."

"Computer design? That doesn't sound like you."

"I'm not doing feng shui anymore. I need to broaden my services."

"Great." Tess hesitated, still unsettled by her sister's decision to abandon a natural talent in favor of something more mainstream. But they'd already argued that one and she wasn't about to drag it out again. "So, have you heard from Ryan?"

Erin's shoulders tensed. "No, and I don't expect to. I told you before I don't want to talk about it."

"Right, I'm sorry. It's just that you two seemed to hit it off so well."

"Look." Erin stopped and turned to her. "I'm not like you. I don't want to discuss every detail of my love life, or lack thereof."

"I'm sorry—"

"It's okay." She held up her hand before Tess could respond. "Really. It's me. I've been a little out of it lately. I didn't mean to snap at you."

"I know what you mean. I've been feeling a little…I don't know, disconcerted, myself lately."

Erin frowned. "Really? You?"

"Yeah. Why not me?"

"You always seem to have it so together."

"I can't figure it out. Everything's going well. The nursery's turning a nice profit. Mason's the bomb. I can't find anything specific to complain about. I just— You know, I'm with my guys and I get so frustrated sometimes."

"You and me both." Erin rolled her eyes.

"I know they're a lot to put up with. You really have been a sport. But…it isn't them. They're great. It's…me." She inhaled a deep breath. "Like something's missing."

Erin cocked her head. "So much of your life is wrapped up in your guys. Maybe you're feeling the need to move beyond that."

Move beyond her guys? Tess frowned. "What do you mean?"

"I don't know, maybe life for you shouldn't be all about the men."

"But my life isn't just about them." She had her job. True, she wasn't as passionate about her work as either of her sisters, but that didn't mean anything. Did it? Besides, what was wrong with focusing her energy on her gift?

"Well, thanks for all the help. You'll let me know when you get the rest?" Erin asked.

"Sure, I'll let you know."

"Great. I'll be working late again tonight, so don't worry about me. I'll have my cell on if you need anything."

"Okay. I'll hold down the fort then."

Erin nodded, then climbed up into the passenger seat of the cab. Tess walked toward Thomas, who was saying his goodbyes to Evan.

"Guess it's time to go," Thomas said as he packed away his pipe.

"Hey, Tess, what's up with Erin?" Evan nodded toward the cab. "She didn't even say hello."

"Don't take it personally, Evan. I think she just has a lot on her mind lately."

Thomas scooped his arm around Tess's shoulders. "What do you think is troubling her?"

"I don't know. I asked about Ryan."

Evan and Thomas cringed in unison.

"I know. I know. I don't know what I was thinking. It's still a touchy subject. Why couldn't I have left well enough alone?" Frustration spiked through her. She had to shake off her own funk and focus on helping her sister. That was what big sisters did.

Thomas shook his head. "Don't worry about it, hon. She'll get over it. She always does."

"No, she doesn't. Don't you see? That's the problem. She just holds on to stuff—like this Ryan thing. Maybe I should get Max to talk to him. He's the one responsible for those two hooking up in the first place. Maybe he can find out what really happened."

"And how do you think Erin will feel about that?" Evan asked.

He was right. Erin would be livid if Tess had one of her guys talk to the man who had sent her into a tailspin not so long ago. She sighed. "I just want to know she's going to be all right."

The blue of Thomas's eyes pierced her. "If I'm not mistaken, you have enough on your plate right now to keep you plenty busy."

"Yeah, I hear you're planning some big ball or something," Evan said.

"A ball?" Thomas's eyebrows rose in interest. "Are we all invited?"

"You bet. The entire family will get invitations. The more the merrier. In fact, that gives me a great idea." She kissed Thomas on his cheek. "Thanks. I need to talk to Erin before you take off."

The truck's horn blared. Erin waved at Thomas to hurry up.

Thomas touched Tess's arm. "Think you may have to hold that thought."

Tess nodded, but excitement raced through her a moment later as she waved goodbye. Why hadn't she thought of it sooner?

Of course, she should probably clear it with the planning committee first, but she'd help Erin boost her business a little, help Mason with his project and maybe get back in her sister's good graces. It was perfect.

She'd hire Erin to decorate the ball.

7

TESS PULLED into her apartment complex that night. She'd worked late ordering Erin's special trees and inputting the latest shipment into the computer. She sighed with relief as she exited her car.

Home.

As much as she'd enjoyed her weekend with Mason, it would be good to sleep in her own bed again. Yawning, she climbed the short flight of stairs to her apartment. She'd get Ramon to heat up one of his specialties, maybe the chicken alfredo or some of that pork roast he'd cooked the other night. Her mouth watered with the possibilities. Josh would pour her a glass of wine and Max would draw her a bubble bath.

She pulled her house key from her bag, already feeling better. She'd missed her guys. How had they fared without her? She should have called to let them know she was going to be late. Then again, they might not have noticed. They were probably watching Monday night football.

She opened the door and stopped, staring at the dark living room. This was strange. Where was everyone? She flipped on the light and moved into the apartment. "Hello. Anyone here?"

The refrigerator kicked on, humming softly in the quiet apartment. She stood for a moment, staring at the blank TV screen. When was the last time she'd come home to an empty place?

She dropped her purse on the couch and her pulse quickened. Had something happened? Had one of her guys been hurt and the rest rushed him to the hospital? She turned to look at the phone, but no message light blinked. She pulled out her cell phone and flipped it open. Maybe she'd missed a call. She was always forgetting to charge the darn thing.

Her battery indicator displayed two bars, low, but sufficient, and her message box was empty. Not a single call?

Shaking her head, she dialed Ramon's number. He answered on the third ring. She gripped the phone. "Ramon, what's going on? Where is everyone?"

"Tess? Hi, sweetheart. What do you mean? I was watching the game with my new honey."

"Oh. Are the rest of the guys there?"

"No, just the two of us. You okay?"

She gave a small laugh. "I'm fine. I'm just a little surprised. I came home and no one's here. It's not quite the same."

"Erin's working late again?"

"Yes, she told me earlier she would be. I just thought...well, I thought some of the guys would be here. Someone's always here."

"That is a little strange. There were still a few of them hanging around when I stopped by after work. Now that I think about it, it seems everyone had something to do tonight."

"That makes sense. They all have their own lives now." She picked up the remote control and ran her thumb over some of the buttons, her throat tight. Not that that had ever seemed to matter in the past.

"I left you some salmon cakes in the fridge."

"That sounds great. Thanks, Ramon."

"You want me to come by?"

"No, of course not. You're with your girlfriend. That's good. I'm fine. It'll be nice to have the place to myself for a change. I've forgotten what real privacy is."

"Yeah, you enjoy. I'll call you tomorrow, okay?"

"Sure." Her throat tightened. "You two have a nice evening."

She hung up and the silence buzzed in her ears. What was wrong with her? So her guys were taking a night off. Hadn't she told Erin earlier she was worried about Mason coming by with all of them there? Maybe that wouldn't be a problem now. Maybe she should take advantage and phone him, see what he was doing.

But she put her cell phone away instead of calling him. A night to herself would do her good. She could catch up on her rest, read. As she headed to draw herself a bath, Erin's words drifted back to her.

Maybe life for you shouldn't be all about the men.

Well, tonight it would be about reclaiming a little peace and quiet. She should enjoy the tranquility while it lasted, because sure enough they'd all be back tomorrow.

Surely they would.

The musical notes of her cell phone startled her, disrupting the quiet. Her heart sped as she answered it. "Tess McClellan."

"Hey, beautiful." Mason's voice reached through the line like a caress. "What are you up to tonight?"

A smile bubbled up inside her. "Resting. For some reason I am wiped."

"Must have been a busy weekend."

"I don't recall getting much sleep."

"I won't keep you, then. I know it's short notice, but what are you doing tomorrow night?"

Happiness washed over her. Everything was okay in the world. "You tell me. What *are* we doing tomorrow night?"

"THANKS FOR COMING WITH ME." Mason handed Tess a glass of champagne from a server's passing tray.

Classical music mingled with the conversations of revelers dressed in black dresses and dark suits. Laughter sounded from a nearby group as another white-clad server passed by, bearing a tray of assorted appetizers.

"Thank you for inviting me." Tess set aside her glass and snagged a small cakelike concoction and something that looked like pâté on crackers. "This is a perfect opportunity to talk up Project Mentor and the gala. Besides, I didn't have anything else going on."

"Right. You with the cell phone that doesn't stop ringing and the *friends* who seem to pop out of the woodwork." He closed his mouth, silently cursing himself for the jealousy evident in his words.

She made a show of inspecting the floor around her. "I don't see anyone doing any popping."

"A first." Evidently, she didn't have any *friends* in the medical community. He frowned. Wait, why wasn't she getting any calls? "You didn't bring your cell phone, right?"

She held up the little bag hanging from her wrist as she dabbed a napkin over her lips. "Actually, I did, but no one's calling."

"Have you got it turned on?"

"Yes. They're just not calling." She sipped her champagne, her bottom lip rounding in a sexy pout. "No one but you."

The mournful note in her voice had him frowning even more. Shouldn't he be overjoyed that the competition seemed to be slacking? Yet, somehow he felt a slight outrage on her behalf. "It isn't possible that all your male callers have forgotten you. There must be an issue with your phone."

"No. You got through fine earlier." She sighed and took another sip, perking up slightly to wink at someone behind him.

He turned, scowling. Walter Cousins, an ear, nose and throat specialist, straightened as if he'd been caught stealing, then hurried off to mingle elsewhere. Mason turned back to Tess. "You were flirting with him."

"I winked at him. He was staring. I was just trying to be friendly."

Dismay rose in him. "You would wink at another man while you're here with me as my date?"

"No need to get upset. It isn't like I was making out with him."

"Some men take a wink as an open invitation."

"It wasn't an invitation. It was a…nothing, a harmless little nothing. A hello-thank-you-for-noticing-me."

As she soothed her hand along his arm he stiffened against the sudden impulse to sweep her into his arms and kiss her—to claim her as his before the entire room.

Good God, how could he even think of creating such a spectacle? The place was full of respected colleagues.

He inhaled a calming breath. "It was something to me and I'd appreciate it if you didn't do it anymore."

Her tanned shoulders, bared by the thin straps of her dress, shifted in a movement so erotic, his cock stirred, and he restrained himself from tasting that delicate curve of flesh. Her eyes took on a knowing gleam and she smoothed her hand farther up his arm, bringing her body in close contact with his. "Certainly, Mason. *Anything* you want."

Her hip brushed against him, sending tendrils of heat licking through him. His hand, apparently running independently from his brain, flattened along her lower back and pressed her closer, so the heat of her lovely body melted over his aching cock. He moaned softly in her ear. "You have turned me into a hormonal teen. All you have to do is touch me and I can't think of anything but being inside you."

"We could slip away, find a quiet corner." Her gaze fell to his lips.

"Here? Now?" He stared at her, stunned by her words, but aroused by the image of dragging her into a secluded room, hiking up her dress and taking her against a wall. "They'll be serving dinner soon. We should mingle—promote the ball. People will notice if we're missing."

"So? We'll mingle later."

He pulled back slightly. "Tess, I work with these people."

"And you think none of them have ever snuck off for a quickie?"

"I…it wouldn't be appropriate."

"But it would be fun." She ran her finger along her neckline, drawing his gaze to her breasts. Tiptoeing, she brought her lips to his ear. "There's a reason you don't see any panty lines with this dress. I want you, Mason. Now. I want you hard and throbbing and thrusting deep inside me."

He cursed softly and closed his eyes. "You're a tease, Tess."

Her fingers slipped inside his jacket and traced his nipple through his shirt. Her gaze held him transfixed. "I'm not teasing."

With another silent curse, he took her hand, then threaded his way toward the rear hall, pulling her along with him. The study, it was along here somewhere—yes. He slipped inside the room, relieved to find it deserted.

Tess was in his arms before he could utter a word. Her mouth closed over his and he needed no coaxing as her tongue issued its demand. He cupped her breast and her nipple beaded beneath his palm. Kneading her, he pressed her to the wall and lifted her dress.

Indeed he found no panties to hinder him. Groaning softly into her mouth, he touched her between her legs, blood pounding through his cock as he fingered her wet folds.

She broke the kiss, even as she wrapped one leg around him to give him better access. Her breasts heaved as she laid her head on his shoulder. "Here. I need you inside me now, Mason. Now."

For an instant he stared blankly at the condom she pressed into his hand, then his zipper grated and he hurried to ready himself. "I almost for—"

She impaled herself on him, the heat of her body taking him in, squeezing him, sending his pulse soaring. He lowered his mouth to the same shoulder that had tempted him just moments before and he thrust into her, lost in her scent, the feel of her, the magic that claimed him each time he took her.

"Oh, Mason." Her breath caught and her muscles clenched around him.

The tension inside him coiled and it was all he could do to maintain control. Her moans of pleasure nearly undid him. He gripped her bottom and thrust, gritting his teeth against the primal urge threatening to overpower him.

"Let go, love...oh, harder...yes." Her legs locked around him and she met him stroke for stroke.

He thrust and she stiffened as the first tremors of orgasm hit her. Her muscles tightened around him and he came, the intensity of his own climax nearly draining him. He buckled against her, pinning her between him and the wall.

For long moments all he could do was hold her while his heart pounded and he dragged in lungfuls of air. When at last he pulled back, he found her gazing at him, her eyes dreamy and dark with desire. She had the look of a woman well pleasured. Pride swelled through him and he kissed her, his tongue teasing hers with a newfound playfulness. A lightness filled him and laughter welled up inside him.

As he helped her straighten her dress he couldn't hide his satisfied smile. "Woman, you are going to be the end of me."

"Oh, I don't know." She pulled a pack of wet wipes

from her minipurse, handed him one, then began to clean herself. "I think I'm good for you."

He frowned at the wet wipe. "You planned this whole thing. No panties, a condom and wet wipes in your bag. This was a premeditated seduction."

A contrite smile played along her lips. "Are you complaining?"

The sound of laughter and clinking glasses drifted in through the door. The dinner. He'd completely forgotten where they were. "Not if no one's missed us."

A few moments later, they edged back into the group, just as the party moved into the dining room. Tess squeezed his hand. "Looks like we made it." Her gaze drifted over the buffet spread out at one end of the room. "And boy, have I worked up an appetite."

He scanned the crowd, but no looks of censure passed his way. Maybe their absence had gone undetected. He touched the small of Tess's back and guided her toward the food, nodding greetings to a couple of people as they passed. Tess's eyes rounded as she piled roast beef, sliced chicken and vegetables on her plate, and he smiled at her delight.

Following along behind her, he helped himself to a little bit of everything. When Tess eyed his plate with raised eyebrows, he laughed. "Seems you've finally given me a taste for the good times."

She grinned. "Wonderful, then we'll feast on the banquet of life."

After their plates were as full as they could get them, he pulled out a chair for her at a table beside Walter Cousins. Tess again winked at the man and he laughed. "You've got a live one there, Davies."

"That I do," Mason said, smiling. He met Tess's gaze, and the warmth in her eyes heated him through and through. At least for now she was his and he meant to make the best of it.

SLIGHTLY DISCORDANT NOTES drifted from a distance as Tess entered the open lobby area of the Highlands Oak Park recreational building that Thursday night. The clack of pool balls sounded from a games room to her right. A young girl ran ahead of her harried mother, her arms wrapped around a violin case as they rushed down a side hall toward the strains of the unseen orchestra.

"Tess." Mason's unmistakable baritone filtered through the myriad sounds.

Her pulse quickened as he waved to her from across the room. Cassie and another woman from the DCWC stood beside him outside a meeting room door. Tess hurried over to them, glancing in the room to see many more of the DCWC members already seated in rows of chairs.

"Hi," she said, her gaze warm on Mason.

"Hi." His gaze lingered on her mouth. "Glad you could make it."

Cassie leaned forward. "We were waiting for you before we started. Where's Josh?"

"He had a conflict. I would have been here sooner, but traffic was a bear."

"I got tons of calls and e-mails from members wanting to help," Cassie said. "Isn't that wonderful?"

Tess nodded. "Before we start, I wanted to talk to you about something," she said. "My sister's an interior designer and she would be a shoo-in for the decorations.

I'm sure I could get her to do everything at cost, just for the exposure."

"That sounds great. I'll have the decorating committee give you a call to get her contact information. Oh, Tess, this is Pam Alberts. I'm not sure if the two of you have met."

Tess took the woman's offered hand. "I don't think we've officially met, but your face is familiar from the DCWC luncheon. Thank you for coming to work with us."

"It's my pleasure. I'm so glad our group has decided to help."

"I can't believe this turnout. It's really amazing," Tess said, gesturing toward the room.

Cassie glanced at Mason. "Evidently April made a few calls and explained that she may have been wrong to withhold her support."

"Is she here?" Tess again scanned the room.

"No," Cassie said, but made no further comment.

"Ladies, shall we?" Mason held the door for them.

They filed in and he ushered them into seats at a table facing the rest of the room. "Good evening, everyone," he addressed the group. "First of all, I want to thank you for coming tonight. Your support is heartfelt."

Mason turned to Cassie. "We have a lot to do, and Cassie and Tess have already laid out much of the groundwork, so I will turn things over to them."

Mason slipped into the seat beside Tess and squeezed her hand under the table as Cassie stood. His excitement flowed through Tess and for that one moment the void in her life seemed to shrink.

"I have good news," Cassie began. "I did some calling around and I found a ballroom that will serve well for this purpose." She went on to give the specifics. "They normally book up a year in advance. However, we were extremely fortunate they had a cancellation. It's a tight squeeze, but we can do it."

"How long do we have, Cassie?" Tess asked.

"Just a little over four weeks. We're scheduled for November 5."

The room burst into chatter. Tess glanced at Mason, eyebrows raised. "Did you know about this?"

He patted her hand and his confidence soothed her. "We can do it. I've seen these women work before. If anyone can pull it off, the DCWC can."

"Ladies." Cassie called them back to order as she passed handouts to those seated in the front row. "Please pass these back. I've outlined a time line with action items."

Mason handed one of the papers to Tess, glancing over her shoulder as she scanned it. "Looks like she's got it all in hand," he whispered.

The timeline listed committees, with columns of names along the bottom and each committee's assigned tasks listed in the calendar portion. It did indeed appear as if Cassie had taken care of everything. Tess turned to Mason, frowning. "My name isn't even on here."

He squinted at the page. "Here you are," he said, pointing to a small square at the bottom listing contact info. "Isn't that your cell phone number?"

"It is, but I'm listed after all of Cassie's information. She'll be the main contact and I'm not on any of the committees."

Cassie again addressed the group. "Now, though we have a communications committee, everyone can help spread the word." She motioned to Pam. "You all know Pam is a PR pro and she'll be heading that committee, since she's got connections with all the media."

Raising her hand, Tess said, "Yes, let's talk about marketing. I have a few media connections and some experience with press releases."

"That's great, Tess." Pam stood with a handful of papers she, too, passed out. "I'll send press releases to my usual sources. Here's a list of those sources, along with a copy of the release I've drafted. Please proof these and let me know of any changes. Tess, my e-mail is at the bottom. You can send me any new resources you have that aren't on my list."

She turned back to the rest of the group. "You'll also see there's a flyer on the event that you can post in your neighborhood clubhouses, local libraries and such."

"You know the drill." Cassie clapped her hands. "Let's break down into our respective groups and make this a working session." She directed the committees into different sections of the room.

"Where do I go?" Tess turned to Mason, disappointment filling her. "I don't think they need me."

"Tess, you are the most important person here. Without you, none of this would be happening."

"Exactly, but now these women are so…so…efficient. I'm still the outsider. I get to proof the press release and pass out flyers, along with everyone else."

"Tell you what. A bunch of the teens are wanting to help. Why don't you organize them as volunteers? There's always a million little things that need doing. They can help with that and you can act as a liaison between them and the DCWC."

"Really? You think that'll work?"

"I don't see why not. You can meet them on Saturday at the beach cleanup. Let's talk to Cassie about it."

He moved off to speak with Cassie and Tess glanced around at the groups of women, already busy planning the gala. At least Cassie had liked her idea of having Erin do the decorations. Tess shook her head. She probably shouldn't feel left out. These women were all used to working together. She just had to show them what she had to offer.

Maybe coordinating Mason's teens was just the way for her to do that. A feeling of foreboding stole over her, but she nudged it aside. She'd faced the DCWC and was winning them over. Surely she'd do fine with the teens.

8

By Friday the relentless heat had abated with the help of a massive storm that moved through, drenching Miami's autumn landscape. After pulling a few strings, Tess managed to get Erin's special-order items delivered in record time.

Now that she had her plan squared away with the DCWC, she could talk to Erin. The excitement from the other day raced through Tess as she dialed her sister's cell phone.

Erin would be thrilled with the prospect of getting in on what they hoped would be the hottest event of the fall. With luck, notices of Mason's gala would soon hit the local society pages of the newspapers. According to Josh, who kept his finger on Miami's social pulse through his work as a personal trainer, the elite was already abuzz with news of the ball. He'd even convinced one of his clients, who wrote for one of the papers, to do a write-up on Project Mentor.

Erin's phone rang into her voice mail and Tess growled her frustration. That girl was getting too elusive. "Hey, Erin, it's me. I've got the rest—"

A beep signaled an incoming call. Smiling, she noted Erin's number on her caller ID and clicked over. "I was just leaving you a message."

"Sorry, I'm having a fabric crisis with one of my suppliers. I'm giving them one more chance to get it straight."

"What kind of crisis?"

"It's not so difficult. I want what I ordered to be delivered when promised."

"Of course you do, sweetie."

"So what's up, Tess? I'm a little busy."

"I've got the rest of your order in. Evan can have it all loaded in a flash and I can deliver it straight away, if that works for you."

"That's great. Let me see, I think I can finish up here, then make it to the duplex to meet you in about an hour. Will that work?"

"Perfect."

"Do you have the address?"

She checked the invoice, confirming the street name. "Got it. I'll meet you there."

"You're not going to have Evan deliver it?"

"No, he can hold down the fort here. I do have something I want to talk to you about, if you think you'll have a minute or two."

"That depends." Suspicion laced her voice. "What's it about?"

"Something I hope you'll be excited about. I'll explain when I get there."

"All right, but I really am busy. I picked up a new client this morning. They're neighbors of Nikki's in Coral Gables. They have this huge place. They want to redo their entire interior and they want it done in a month's time to celebrate their golden wedding anniversary."

"You've managed something like that before."

"Not while I was working two other jobs."

"Want to borrow Evan? He doesn't have your eye for design, but he makes a great assistant. I've got him practically running this place when I'm not here. Oh, or Josh, he has a flare of his own."

"I'll think about Josh. For a straight guy he does have an eye for detail. Thanks."

"I'll give him a call right now."

As Tess disconnected, she bit her lip. The ball was just over a month away. Hopefully, Erin's schedule would be clear enough for her to design the gala's decor. She'd know just the touch they needed.

Tess found Evan a few moments later loading some shrubs into a customer's car and waited until he bid the woman goodbye. As the car drove off he turned to her. "What's up, boss? Erin ready for the rest of her stuff?"

"Yep. Can you load up the van for me?"

"You don't want me to make the delivery?"

"Would you mind watching the shop for me? I need to talk to her."

"Right." He cocked his head. "You're going to ask her to use her golden touch on your ball, right?"

"You always read me so well. I'm hoping she'll have time. I hate to admit it, but now that she's gone more mainstream her business seems to be really picking up."

"That's a great idea—to have her do the decorating, that is. I'll bet she goes for it. It's a great way for her to showcase her abilities to the right folks. Josh called, by the way."

"Great. I'll give him a call now. I need to talk to him, too." She turned to leave.

"Hey, Tess."

She turned back. "Yes?"

"You look good."

"Oh, thanks, Evan."

"No, really. I mean you always look good. But there's something different about you these days."

His gaze traced her body with the knowing eye of a former lover, but the warmth in his eyes reflected nothing more than the deep fondness she shared with all her exes. "It's like you have this glow about you. Must be the new man."

"Oh, well…thanks."

He stood staring at her, an unreadable expression on his face. "He's different, isn't he?"

She inhaled a deep breath. "Yes, I guess he is."

"Yeah, I can tell, because you're different."

"Am I?" She took a step closer to him. "How so?"

His broad shoulders lifted in an easy shrug. "Hard to say. It's just that you haven't quite been yourself lately, I guess, and now suddenly you seem to have this new excitement about you."

"Really?" She didn't feel so excited. She felt drained. She'd been having trouble sleeping lately. "I've missed everyone this week. The apartment has been really quiet."

"Has it? I had to help a friend move. None of the other guys have been there?"

"No. The place is so…deserted."

"I'll bet it is. Must be nice for a change."

She shrugged. "Guess I've just gotten used to having everyone around."

"You okay?"

"Oh, sure."

"I promised my brother I'd do something with him tonight, but I'll bet a bunch of the others will stop by." He rubbed his hand along the back of his head. "I can't ever remember a time when I've been there and there weren't at least three or four of the others there, too."

"I know. It's strange. Probably just a weird coincidence that everyone else had something to do this week."

"That's probably it."

"There's not anything going on that I don't know about, is there?"

He shook his head. "Not that I'm aware of."

"Okay, but you would tell me, right, if there was?"

"Sure, but like what?"

"Like if all the guys were upset with me, or didn't want to hang with me anymore."

A short laugh burst from him. "That would never happen."

"Well, you don't know."

"No, not with you, Tess. Maybe with some other chick, but you're one of a kind. You make a guy feel like he's worth something. Who's ever going to give that up?"

"Eventually, everyone does move on." Sadness filled her.

"Don't sweat it. You're still all that."

"Thanks. I'm not so sure I'm ready for all of you to desert me just yet, but I suppose a little breathing room wouldn't do me any harm."

"It's all good, though I wouldn't count on a mass exodus anytime soon."

She laughed, though her heart wasn't in it. It seemed the exodus had already started. Putting on a brave front, she smiled. "Oh, wouldn't Erin freak? She'd think you were all wiped from the earth by some plague or something."

"Now, that one would be happy to see a little less of us."

"Actually, I don't think she minds. She's hardly there anymore. She's buried in her business." She leaned over and kissed his cheek. "Thanks, Evan."

"Sure. Now, I'd better get loading. I know how happy she gets when her special orders come in."

"That she does."

He headed for the greenhouse where they'd stored Erin's special-order items. Tess frowned at his retreating back. A sense of apprehension swept over her. What if her guys were truly moving on?

Would she be ready to let them go?

"Josh?" Tess pressed her ear to her cell phone and glanced at the directions she'd downloaded to the duplex where Erin was working.

"Tess, what's up?"

"Not much. So sorry I missed my workout Sunday."

"Yeah, right." His voice took on a teasing tone. "After all the heated looks passing between you and the good doctor, I got the feeling you were having a different kind of workout."

She cleared her throat. "Hey, listen, I have a favor to ask you."

"You're changing the subject, but shoot."

"Well, you know how we've all been a little concerned about Erin lately?"

"Of course, love, your worries are our worries."

"I have this idea of how you can help and put your

talents to good work at the same time." She outlined her plan for him to assist Erin over the coming month with her multiple design contracts.

"And while I'm working with her, you want me to get a feel for what's been bugging her."

"Hey, you said that, not me. Let's keep the record straight here. Of course, it's not a bad idea. Your schedule's flexible. You could work with her, befriend her, gain her confidence. You always know the right thing to say."

"You want me to report everything I learn back to you."

"Well, I *would* like to know what you learn—"

"So you can meddle in your sister's life."

"I do not meddle. I'm worried about her. I want to know what's wrong so I can help her. I just can't seem to talk to her. I always say the wrong thing."

"I'll make you a deal. I'll lend a hand with her design projects as my schedule allows, and if she warms to me more on a personal basis, we'll play things by ear."

"No pressure. It would be great if you'd just do whatever you feel you can do."

"I'll report to you if and when I feel it's reasonable for you to know and Erin would be comfortable with you knowing."

"You can't ask her outright, she'll say no, even though I always have her best interest at heart. She's a younger sister. They don't ever appreciate that."

"*I* will make all determinations about any information that needs to be gathered or passed on. You have to consider that there may be ample reason for her to keep her personal life to herself."

"Okay, but if for some reason you learn something

of importance and you're not sure about telling me, you have to promise to tell Nikki."

A short silence sounded across the connection. "I'll think about that, but no promises."

"Great. Thanks, Josh."

"So what happened at the last planning meeting? I'm sorry I missed it, but I talked the gala up to my client. We just need to let him know when. He's a big flooring guy—lots of money and a wife with a big heart who likes to spend it."

"Sounds like our kind of people. We do have a date set—Saturday, November 5."

He whistled softly. "That's cutting it close."

"I know, but we're lucky to have that. These places book up way in advance. I know Nikki said she barely worked her wedding reception in for February. We wouldn't have gotten that ballroom so soon, if not for a cancellation. Cassie was smart to jump on it. Anyway, we're meeting at the same place and time every Thursday until the gala. We figured we'd need to meet at least once a week to pull this off, though I have to admit the DCWC seems to have it all under control."

"How come you don't sound happy about that?"

"I am. It's going to be great. I'm unofficially meeting some of Mason's teens tomorrow. They want to help with the planning and I'm going to coordinate them volunteering with the DCWC."

A short silence spun across the line. "That'll be interesting."

"What does that mean?"

"Nothing. You'll be great with them. How could they not love you? The rest of us do."

She frowned, trying to scan the deeper meaning behind his words, but drawing a blank. That was odd. "All right, I'm on my way to see Erin now. I'll have her give you a call."

"Sounds good. And Tess?"

"Yes?"

"I really think Mason is a great guy and he's going to be good for you...but you need a little time to chill. You haven't quite been yourself lately, girlfriend, and the last thing you need is to take on any more stress."

"What stress? I'm not stressing."

"Just think about it before you jump into something really serious with this guy."

Something serious? Again she tried to scan his emotions, but came up empty. What the hell?

"Josh, I don't know what everyone is getting all twisted up about. You know how it goes. I'm with Mason now, but that doesn't mean it's anything serious. This encounter will be no more and no less serious than any of my previous encounters have been."

"Okay, but you do know the rest of the group want to meet him. I've reassured them as much as I can, but—"

"Look, I can't take this right now. I'll talk to you later, okay?"

"You've got it, love. Just so you know, Dr. Davies is okay by me."

"Thanks, Josh, I appreciate that."

She said goodbye, then disconnected as she pulled up to the delivery address on Erin's invoice. "What was all the fuss about? Was there something going on that she was missing?

And why hadn't she been able to read Josh?

"THIS IS GREAT, TESS. Thanks for delivering these. If I can tie up this project over the next week or so, I should be in good shape." Erin fluffed the leaves on the last ficus they'd unloaded.

"Be sure to give Josh a call. You know, not only does he have a good eye, but he's very well connected. He'd be one to foster a relationship with. You never know when one of his clients will need an interior decorator."

"Remember that's all I'm doing these days. No more of that alternative stuff. I'm busier than ever since I gave up the feng shui."

"Again, I can't stress what a shame that is—"

Erin held up her hand. "I'm not getting into that again with you."

"Okay, not a problem."

"I hope that isn't what you came here to talk to me about."

"No, this is really good. I hope you'll be as excited about it as I am."

"Excited about what?"

Tess inhaled a deep breath. "You know I mentioned that Mason, this new guy I'm seeing, is involved with this nonprofit group?"

"Oh, right, that was part of that gushing bit the other day."

"I wasn't gushing."

"Whatever. So he's involved with a nonprofit?"

"Right, Project Mentor. It helps kids who come from families of misfortune, mostly victims of drug and alcohol abuse. Usually their parents or a caretaker is or was a user the group finds through their free clinic."

"That's so sad."

"I know. I couldn't believe it when the DCWC wasn't going to help him."

"The DCWC?"

"The Dade County Women's Club. I mentioned them the other day."

"No you didn't."

"I thought I did when I told you and Thomas about the fund-raiser. Mason had broken off his engagement to the president and she was none too happy about it. She—"

"The point, Tess, get to the point. I'm on a tight schedule here."

"The DCWC is helping him organize a big fund-raiser to drum up money for a youth center where they can have regular programs for these kids. We're holding a gala, the event of Miami's—"

"Yeah, I think I've heard about that— Wait a minute. Back up. What do you mean *we're* holding a gala?"

"That's what I was saying. The DCWC is helping Project Mentor with the fund-raiser."

"You mean to tell me you're part of this women's group?" Erin's eyebrows arched.

"That's right." Tess straightened, lifting her head high as irritation grated through her. "I am the newest member of the Dade County Women's Club and I—"

"You?" The corners of Erin's mouth twitched. "You joined a women's club?"

"Yes, and I—"

"That's where you met this guy? At this women's club?"

"He was there making a plea for help and they weren't going to help him, because—"

"Wait. I don't get it. What were you doing joining a women's club in the first place?"

"Don't look so amused. I'm a woman. Why can't I join a woman's club? There's no law against it. Why are you grinning? I fail to see what's so funny."

"I'm sorry." Erin made a feeble attempt to hide her amusement. "It's just hard to picture. Do you all wear little white gloves and drink tea with your pinkies out?"

"No. Don't be silly, Erin. All I wanted was to get involved in some charitable activities and make some new friends."

For some reason this information tickled her sister all the more. She laughed. "Wait. Are you telling me you found this group so you could make friends with some of the women and you stole the president's fiancé?"

"Ex-fiancé. And I did not steal him."

"Same difference. You scooped him up right from under their noses." She shook her head. "Probably not the best way to make new friends. You are your own worst enemy."

Tess rolled her eyes in frustration. "It isn't like I did it on purpose."

"I'm sorry, Tess. I know you didn't. I'm a little jealous of the way men flock to you. I can't help it that I find some satisfaction in your charms backfiring on you. I can't wait to tell Nikki."

"She already knows and she did *not* think it was funny. She yelled at me."

"Yelled at you? What for?"

Tess shrugged, embarrassed by her initial response to Mason's request for help. "Well, I figured they must have had a good reason not to help with the fund-raiser.

And like I just said, I needed to *do* something and to find some girlfriends to hang with. You and Nikki are all so wrapped up in your own stuff and I was on testosterone overload. I was dying for female companionship and if I spoke up—I wasn't even an official member at the time—I knew I'd be blowing whatever shot I had at connecting with those women."

Erin stared at her, frowning, all signs of her good humor gone. "Why didn't you say something? You would rather join a bunch of strangers in a women's group than tell me or Nikki that you wanted some girl time?"

"I never said I preferred it. Nikki is wrapped up in her new life with Dylan and you…"

Erin's lips thinned. "And I what?"

"You're so hard to talk to these days. See, look at how you're getting angry—"

"That's rich. You do something silly like join some women's club and it's my fault because you can't do something as simple as talk to me?"

"I never said anything was your fault and they are nice women—"

"And how many friends have you made since you stole the president's fiancé? That is so like you. There's a man around and you can't wait to get your hands on him."

"Ex-fiancé and that is so wrong, Erin. How can you say that?"

"Because it's true. It's exactly what Maggie would have done. I can't believe you did this, Tess. What could you have been thinking?"

Anger flashed through Tess. "Why do you always have to be so down on her—so down on me? What is wrong with me wanting some new friends? You should be thrilled that I'm spending a little time away from all my guys."

"You practically ignore me, because you're so caught up in all your men. I tolerate having them underfoot all the time, but when you want a little female companionship, do you ask me if *I'm* available?"

"You haven't exactly been available lately."

"Maybe I would have made myself available. Did you ever think of that?"

Tess stared at her. "No."

"Right. So, how many new friends did you say you've made with this group?"

Anger and hurt warred in Tess, but she'd be damned if she let Erin see how upset she was. "I've made one acquaintance. She's helping with the ball, which I convinced them to support after all."

"One acquaintance. Good for you, Tess. Give yourself some brownie points."

Tess raised her chin. Why had she thought Erin would want to help? She must have been hallucinating when she dreamed that one up. "I didn't join just for that. I wanted to be involved in something…important. I'm sorry I got you all riled up. I asked Josh to call you."

"Fine. Thanks."

With a shake of her head, Tess left. She certainly hadn't expected that kind of response from her sister. She punched in her mother's number on her cell phone, but the call went into voice mail and she hung up.

Maggie was probably neck-deep into a good time right now. Why bother her? Maybe it would be better to talk to someone who would have some good sound advice. Who better than Aunt Sophie?

9

"I DON'T KNOW, AUNT SOPHIE, it's like the world has gone mad."

"Here, hon, have some tea." Her aunt handed her a cup of the warm brew she'd poured from a tray set on the table in her sunroom.

"Thanks." Tess took a tentative sip. One never knew exactly what Sophie might be serving, but she always had exactly the blend to soothe whatever ailment one brought to her doorstep.

"That's nice." Tess took a longer sip. "What is that? Peach?"

"With a little something extra."

"There's always something extra."

"It's all these simple pleasures that make life worth living."

"That's something you always do so well."

Sophie's eyebrows rose in question. "Make tea?"

"Enjoy the simple pleasures. Exactly how is it you do that? Everything I do seems to get so…complicated."

"Let me see…first, you have to make time for the simple things, like taking a long soak in the tub, or having tea with your favorite aunt."

"You're my only aunt and, yes, this is nice, but I see

you're probably right about taking the time. Seems like I don't do much of that."

"No, you don't. You're all caught up in the big things—this new love affair, the fund-raiser, your relationship with Erin. You need time every day to put all that aside and have a quiet moment. It can be a nice cup of tea, or a walk on the beach, or just watching the sunset. You can do these things alone or with someone else, but the key is to revere the experience."

Tess nodded. "You make it sound so easy."

"It is easy, dear. That's why they're the simple pleasures."

"So what do I do about Erin? And I'm not so sure I like this whole…whatever is going on with my guys, and what if Mason really is different like everyone seems to think? What does that mean, exactly?"

Sophie chuckled softly. "One at a time. You don't need to do anything about Erin. These things work themselves out." She shrugged. "You could give her a little time to cool off, then invite her to dinner or to see a movie. She's just gotten her feelings hurt. It hasn't been easy for her being your younger sister, you know. You've always had this whirlwind of activity going on around you. It isn't a bad thing, though you do tend to get too caught up in some of the drama. I'm sure she feels a little lost in the shuffle is all."

"Really? I guess I never thought of things that way."

"It's easier to see from the outside and it's wonderful entertainment for the rest of us."

"Thanks. I never realized I was providing the show."

"Just part of it."

Tess took a long sip, relaxing into the soft cushions.

"Okay, so what about all my guys? I know I was getting frustrated, but if I go home tonight to an empty apartment again I'm going to feel a little depressed."

"Won't Erin be there?"

"She'll be working late again. And you think she'll be talking to me, anyway?"

"Could be."

"I think I may have set myself up for this when I started the whole needing-more-in-my-life thing, but I never meant for my guys not to want to hang around."

"It's possible you're experiencing some kind of shift in your gift."

"Shift? What kind of shift?"

"I'm not sure. Like I've said before, you girls are a new breed. The gift tends to manifest a little differently in each of us, and I think with your generation it seems to have evolved."

"And this shift, you think it's changing…like I've lost my touch or something and so my guys are drifting away?"

"I don't think you can just lose your abilities. That healing energy must remain, but changes somehow."

"How? A week ago I couldn't turn around without bumping into one of my guys. Today I'm feeling a little deserted." She pulled out her cell phone. "Look, no messages. No calls. That never happens."

"Maybe."

Tess sat forward. "It's more than that." A bluebird glided past the floor-to-ceiling windows overlooking her aunt's garden. "I can't feel them anymore."

"What do you mean, dear?"

She turned her gaze to her aunt. "It's kind of like it suddenly got quiet, but I hadn't noticed that it was loud before. Like there was this underlying sound in the background that I didn't hear, but now it's gone."

"You're speaking of your empathic abilities?"

"That's right. I can't explain it, but I have this feeling that they're gone." She took a deep breath to stem the anxiety rising in her. Until she'd admitted her fears aloud, they hadn't seemed real. "I tried to scan Josh earlier when we were on the phone—I've always been able to do that. Sometimes even remotely with a current lover, nothing really strong, but there was that connection. But today...nothing."

"And with your new man, this doctor, is it the same?"

"The same as what? It's been different with him from the start. He makes me feel so...I don't know...alive. It's like I've always sensed emotions with the others, but it's different with him. It's more like I really *feel* what he's feeling. Do you ever get that? When we make love it's the most fantastic experience."

"Like double the pleasure?"

"Yes, and because I enjoy it so much more, he seems to enjoy it more and it's this incredible circuit of feeling. The high is really high, like nothing I've ever experienced."

She leaned closer to her aunt. "I don't know exactly how, but somehow it is different than with the others. What does that mean? That my gift is changing?"

Sophie's eyes narrowed. "Could be it's all concentrating around this one man as opposed to spreading out over all your men. I don't know that I've heard of anything like this happening before, but I do believe that Nikki will stay with Dylan and that will be a first."

"But she loves him like none of the others. And she's given up her gift, hasn't she?"

"I'm not so sure, but this is uncharted territory. How would she tell she's lost her gift if she's only with a man she has already healed? She's not exactly putting it to the test, so to speak. Could it be that her gift has also evolved?"

"Whatever's going on, she's happy. I saw her last week and she was practically glowing."

"Kind of the way you do when you talk about your new young man?"

"See? You're not the first to say that. What does that mean? Does it mean I'll stay with Mason the way Nikki stayed with Dylan and that I'll risk losing my gift, too?" As much as Tess cared for Mason, the thought brought a wave of anxiety crashing over her.

"I don't know, dear, but I'm sure it's nothing to be concerned about. The best you can do is to be clear on what you're feeling and act accordingly. You'll know when the time is right if you need to move on or not. It certainly isn't something you have to decide right now."

The sense of foreboding in Tess heightened, twisting in her stomach. "But you do see it as a possibility, then—that I might stay with him, for always, that I might lose my gift and all my other men?"

Sophie nodded toward Tess's forgotten cup. "Drink. It'll calm you. I'm saying I don't know. You'll know when the time is right. Have you ever questioned when it was time to move on in the past?"

"No."

"There. So there's no reason to believe you'll have trouble now. This could just be a case where you've met a man who needs more healing, so he's drawing these extra-intense emotions from you."

"You think so?"

"It could be. Maybe you'll just be with him that much longer while all these feelings level out, or maybe you're experiencing a condensed version of your earlier encounters and it will all wind up in a couple of months as usual."

"So maybe these feelings will ease eventually and I'll be back to my old self?"

"It isn't for me to say." Sophie lifted the teapot from the tray. "We've sucked all this down. I'll go make some more."

The musical notes of Tess's cell phone sounded as Sophie left the room. "Hello?"

"Tess, this is Victoria."

"Victoria, is everything all right?"

"Everything's fine. I just got here a little while ago, but Evan is still here. I'm calling to let you know you have a visitor. Evan thought you'd be back by now and I wasn't sure if I should have him wait."

Tess's heart quickened. "What kind of visitor? Who is it?"

"His name is Mason Davies. He said you weren't expecting him. Should I ask him to come back? Evan's talking to him. He seemed really interested in meeting him. Is he a customer?"

"No, he's not a customer. Well…I guess he could be." Anticipation rippled through Tess. Mason had come to see her.

"Tell him I'll be there in about twenty minutes and ask him if he can wait." She hung up and slung her purse over her shoulder. "Aunt Sophie," she called, walking toward the kitchen.

Sophie turned, teapot in hand, a knowing smile on her face. "Go on, sweetheart. Enjoy your young man."

Tess drew up. "How did you know?"

"Oh, it's obvious, sweetheart. You're as lit up as a Christmas tree." She nodded thoughtfully. "No doubt about it, this one's special."

Excitement and uncertainty swirled through Tess. "Yes, I guess he is."

She hugged her aunt, then hurried out the door. Traffic had already slowed with the onset of the evening rush hour, but she maneuvered the best she could, slipping onto back roads at her first opportunity. A traffic light ahead of her turned red and she stopped, drumming her fingers impatiently.

Could Sophie be right? Could it be that her gift was evolving? A chill ran through her. "Oh, God, please don't let me be losing my gift."

The light changed and she moved ahead, only to be stopped a block later. The knot of unease that had settled in her stomach earlier tightened. She couldn't lose her gift. She was a healer. If she lost her gift, then who would she be?

Okay, she should try to read Mason. If she could do a remote reading and it came in clearer than in the past, then perhaps Sophie's theory was right. At the next light she closed her eyes and filled her mind with thoughts of him, letting her heart take in whatever emotions came to her.

A sense of curiosity, mixed with excitement came over her. She opened her eyes, breathing deeply as she sorted through the feelings. All right, she was a little excited herself about seeing him, but this didn't seem to be coming from her. Did that mean he was excited at the prospect of seeing her?

What was he curious about?

With another deep breath, she focused again on Mason. Her stomach tightened with a deep sense of unease.

She bit her lip and made the final turn on her way to the nursery, a nervous shiver running up her spine. He was alone at the nursery with Evan. Depressing the accelerator, she sped along the last mile to the shop.

What could the two of them be talking about?

MASON SHIFTED BESIDE Tess's assistant, Evan, whom she'd mentioned on several occasions. They'd apparently known each other for quite some time. What a disappointment that she hadn't been there for him to surprise her.

Hopefully she'd be along shortly, though. Mason brightened. In the meanwhile, Evan would be a fount of information on her.

Gesturing to a low structure along the back of the property, Evan completed his tour. "This building was the original greenhouse. We use it mostly as storage and for special-order items."

"It's a great setup, and Tess has owned this for how long?"

"Let's see, her great-aunt Emma passed maybe two or three years ago. She left a nice little nest egg for each of the girls." He gestured to the complex. "This is what Tess did with hers. We've fixed it up a good bit. Added that front greenhouse. The place was pretty run-down, but it's a good location. It turns a nice profit."

"It suits her. She definitely has a nurturing side."

Evan's eyebrows rose. "Oh, she's a nurturer, all right. I suppose they all are—the McClellan women—but I think our girl may be the most nurturing of them all."

Our girl? So, were they sharing her, then? Surely not in any intimate sense. Tess had been very specific about that each-in-his-own-time thing and this was Mason's time, damn it. "And how long have you known Tess?"

"Four, maybe five years."

"And how did you meet?"

"It was amazing. I used to hate elevators. Couldn't get in one for anything. Used to get claustrophobic." He shook his head. "It was horrible. Anyway, I came home one night—I live in this high-rise, but on the fourth floor—and I always took the stairs—but this one night the stairs were blocked off. They were painting. Can you believe it? I was outraged. What if they had a fire? You can't close down the stairs.

"Anyway, they did have another stairwell way on the other side of the building and I was whipped. Been hauling trusses all day. So I start to drag my butt to the other side of the building and there stands Tess, holding the elevator for me. I'm thinking no way, then she smiles, and, I don't know about you, but there is no way I can deny that woman when she gets that look—you know the look that says she has a plan and she's going to take care of everything and you might as well come along and enjoy yourself."

Yeah, he knew that look. "So, you got on the elevator."

"It was a ride to heaven, if you know what I mean. I

have never had issues with small places ever since. The woman cured me. She's a miracle worker, I'm telling you. She had to be to get me on that elevator in the first place."

Mason gritted his teeth. She'd had sex with a total stranger in an elevator. His stomach tightened. "So, how long were you with her?" His face warmed. "Assuming the two of you are no longer...seeing each other...in that way."

"Oh, no, I've got myself a real honey. We're getting married next spring."

"Good for you." And good for him as well, one less blast from her past to contend with. "Congratulations."

"Thanks. Tess and I were together just a couple months. Some of the best days of my life. She changed me in so many ways. Made me better, stronger. All I know is that I could never have gotten a woman like Jaida without Tess having healed me."

Mason laughed. "Healed you?"

"Oh, yeah." The serious look in Evan's eyes had Mason frowning. "Healed me. No doubt about it. I was a mess before Tess. It wasn't just the claustrophobia. I screwed up every relationship I'd ever been in. That woman has some kind of magic. I know you've felt it."

"Well, maybe, but magic? So she helped you become a better person. That doesn't mean it was magic."

Evan nodded, his face set in a knowing look. "It's still new to you, and I guess since you're a man of medicine it's a little harder for you to accept. But the rest of us, we know how it is."

"The rest of you? Just how many more are there?"

"You know, there's nothing for you to get jealous

about. We've all moved on. Sure, we like to drop in and check on her—take care of anything that needs doing." He stopped and frowned. "Funny, I just realized I haven't seen her outside of work for a while." He shrugged. "Anyway, we all feel like we owe her—not in an obligatory sense. She gives with such an open heart. It's impossible not to want to give back in some way."

"And how long do her relationships last?" Mason wanted to kick himself for asking, but damn it, he had to know.

"It varies. Depends on the guy. A few months on average. You'll know when it's time to move on. You'll be ready. You need to just chill and enjoy your time with her."

Enjoy his time with her? The sick feeling in his gut intensified. Mason inhaled a deep breath to try to bring some clarity to his thinking. Evan believed Tess was some kind of healer. Mason needed to chill and not care about her past. And most important, the clock was ticking on his time with her.

He closed his eyes for a moment. He'd known all this already. Having it confirmed was a bit of a blow, though. Truth was there was something…unique happening with Tess. Magic seemed a bit of a stretch, but whatever it was he didn't feel anywhere near ready to give it up.

You'll know when it's time to move on. You'll be ready.

What if he was never ready?

"You're in luck." Evan clapped him on his back. He nodded to the white van as it pulled into the parking lot. "Here she comes."

Relief and excitement flooded Mason at the sight of Tess emerging from the vehicle. Just seeing her made him feel better. Was that magic? If his days with her were numbered, then he meant to make the most of them. With a backward thanks to Evan he ran to greet her.

Her smile lit her face when she saw him and her beauty nearly took his breath away. How could he have ever thought her anything short of remarkable?

She met him halfway and he swept her into his arms and kissed her before she could utter a word. Her mouth was warm and welcoming, her tongue giving. He couldn't get enough. When she pressed her body close and moved against him, waves of desire shot through him. Unable to restrain himself, he kneaded her breast until she moaned softly into his mouth and stroked her hand over his chest, palming his own nipple into an aching point.

He broke the kiss but let his fingers linger on her breast. "Can you leave with me?"

She nodded, waved to Evan, then practically dragged Mason to his car. Traffic proved to be thankfully light as he maneuvered along I-95 to his house. He should have asked if her apartment was closer.

"Hurry," she murmured as she nibbled at his neck and stroked his thigh.

He half hoped she wouldn't stop there, but he'd be hard put to find a secluded spot along the interstate if they got too carried away. He shook his head. What had she done to him? Before their little tryst during the dinner party the other night he never would have thought such a thing.

Still, she had his shirt wide open and was suckling one nipple while toying with the other by the time they reached the safety of his garage.

"You little minx." He tugged her off him, then made

short work of her buttons, spreading her shirt wide to reveal a very sexy bra. Her breasts tempted him through a film of lace that barely contained them.

"I've been thinking of you nonstop." With a twist of his fingers he released the front clasp on her bra and freed her breasts for his pleasure.

She cupped them and lifted them up to him as he lowered his head. "I've been thinking about you, too. Why did we wait so long? Tuesday was eons ago."

She stilled as his mouth closed over her breast. While he suckled her with abandon, he rolled her other nipple between his thumb and forefinger, eliciting soft whimpering sounds from her that sent his blood pounding.

"Oh, Mason...I love when you do that. It gets me so turned on."

Her fingers threaded through his hair, holding him in place. He settled in and sucked his fill, savoring the feel of her hard nipple against his tongue, the sounds of her heightening excitement and the smell of her musky scent as she shifted, parting her legs in invitation.

Not wanting to disappoint either one of them, he slipped his free hand under the hem of her skirt. Had she purposely dressed again for easy access, or was a short skirt and thong her standard attire?

Her swollen, wet flesh sent all thought from his mind, other than his burning desire to slip inside her. He pushed two fingers into her and was rewarded with a wild groan as she gyrated against him.

She arched, pressing her breast farther into his mouth, and his fingers deeper inside her. His cock hardened and he shifted to relieve some of the pressure. His hip hit the horn. It blared, the sound startling them both.

"Sorry." He pulled back to gaze at her face flushed with desire. "Let's go inside."

A devilish light lit her eyes. "I have a better idea. Follow me."

She moved to slip over the front seat into the back. In the process her bottom came in close proximity to his face and he breathed in the musky scent of her arousal. Acting on impulse, he anchored her as she hung half over the seat, her lovely ass positioned just right for him to take advantage.

"Mason," she gasped in a breathy whisper as he shoved her skirt up.

"If you're going to make me swelter in this car, we're going to have a little fun with it."

She only moaned in answer as he parted her tight buttocks and went straight for her clit. He sucked her swollen flesh into his mouth and pulled hard, as he'd done with her nipples, laving the hard bud until she gasped and bucked against him. Liquid heat seeped from her and he drank his fill, holding her in place with a firm grip on her hips.

He crouched on the front seat and thrust his tongue into her, savoring her salty taste, losing himself in the glory of taking all he wanted from her.

She pushed against him. "Oh, yes...yes."

Excitement rose in him. The need to give to her filled him. Her taste, her scent, triggered something feral in him and he let himself pleasure her the way he'd only imaged doing until now.

Using his lips, tongue and teeth, he experimented, alternating his technique depending on her response. When she shifted, he took her cue and changed the pressure of his tongue, until she moved in steady rhythm against him, her cries of passion growing decidedly wilder, sending his own desire to new heights.

She was hot and willing. Was there anything she'd deny him? His cock was so stiff he wondered briefly if he'd survive, but he was so caught up in her unhindered response. Centering on her clit again he laved her with the point of his tongue, moving in quickening circles as she ground against him, moaning with every gyration of her hips.

Even as he shifted again to relieve the pressure in his groin, she stiffened as the first tremors of her orgasm hit her. He held her fast and continued his assault as her muscles clenched and she screamed her release.

He ran his mouth over her as she calmed, soothing her with gentle strokes of his lips and tongue.

The taste of her.

Only when he'd laved away the last drop, did he pull back to stroke her heavenly ass. The woman didn't have a bad angle. He squeezed one firm cheek, her skin smooth and soft.

"That'll get me started again." She glanced back at him, her breasts exposed and heaving with her exertion.

"Really?"

She shrugged, laughter in her eyes. "Playing with my ass, my breasts, just kissing me the way you do. They all seem to do the trick."

He took her buttocks in his hands and kneaded her. Her eyes grew dark and she pressed back against him again. He licked his lips and met her gaze. "And if you rub your breasts while I stroke your ass, will it get you wet again?"

Her eyes widened and she nodded as she complied, caressing her breasts as he stroked her bottom. "Oh," she said in that breathy voice, "do you have any idea what a turn-on this is?"

"Oh, yes." He unbuttoned his slacks. "How long?"

She laughed, the sound sexy as all get out. "We can do this all day and night if you want."

He grimaced. "I mean how long before you're ready to take me inside you?"

"Oh." Her eyes widened. "Now. Is it too crowded, or can you manage from there?"

"Hold on. Don't move." He dug in the glove box and thankfully found a condom. After readying himself, he reached for the control panel and opened the sunroof, then he rose to his knees on the seat, his head just clearing the small opening as he positioned himself behind her.

"Oh, yes, Mason, now." She pressed back, impaling herself on his cock.

She was wet and tight and he nearly lost control as he again gripped her hips and pulled her back hard on him. Then all he could do was feel as he thrust into her over and over, his gaze fixed on the vision of her tight ass swallowing his cock, her muscles contracting around him, bringing him the most exquisite pleasure he'd ever known.

An unprecedented warmth tightened his throat and expanded his chest to the point it seemed to spill out of him as he closed his eyes and focused on making love to her. That's what this was. Making love. Awe filled him at the realization. So, this was how it felt.

She reached toward him and he took her hand and held on as they continued their loving, their movements fluid, the feel of her intoxicating, the tension coiling to almost unbearable heights.

It had never felt so wild, so good before. He thrusted with abandon, dropping her hand to reach forward and cup her breast. He slipped his other hand between her legs. She straightened with him, until her back pressed against his chest and he groaned at the changing pressure, thrusting upward into her, while he squeezed her nipple and caressed her clit.

She cupped her hands over his and rolled her head back against his shoulder, exposing her neck. He fastened his mouth on her there to stifle the yell rising in him as his body tensed. He sucked in a breath and plunged into her.

The spasms of her orgasm rippled around him and he felt his control slipping. Gritting his teeth, he fought to restrain himself, hating the wild, out-of-control feeling sweeping over him. Her inner muscles tightened and he came, crying out against her neck, in spite of himself.

10

HOURS LATER HE TURNED TO HER, the sight of her hair spread across his pillows bringing a smile to his face. She drew lazy circles along his chest with the tip of her finger. Her eyes, that startling blue, filled with warmth.

"It's okay, you know," she said.

"What's okay?"

"It's okay if you lose control while we're making love."

He hesitated a long moment. "I—I don't want to hurt you."

"Oh, Mason." She cupped his cheek. "You could never do that."

"I wish I could be so sure."

"Have you ever lost control and hurt anyone before?"

He took a deep breath. "I don't lose control. Hey, you hungry? I forgot to feed you."

"I'm okay. Please don't change the subject. I want to talk about this."

Anger rose in him. "What's wrong? Is my lovemaking too restrained for you? 'Cause you didn't seem to be complaining." The minute the words left his mouth he felt three times an ass. "I'm sorry, babe. That was uncalled-for."

Her hand was smooth and warm as she pressed it to his chest. A blanket of calm soothed over him. He closed his eyes. "Sometimes, it seems I have all this…" He motioned lamely, not sure what he meant to say, not sure why he was saying it. "Maybe I have too much bottled up inside me."

"It has to come out sometime. You do know that, right?"

He opened his eyes and met her gaze. "Evan says you healed him."

Her hand flexed against him. "Did he?"

"Yes."

"I wondered what the two of you talked about." She resumed drawing circles on his chest.

He stilled her hand. "Is that what you're doing here? Trying to analyze me so you can heal me or something?"

The blue of her eyes seemed as bottomless as the sea. "I am a healer, Mason. Me, my mother, my sisters, all the McClellan women before me and, I assume, all to come after me."

He stared at her, not quite sure what to make of her quiet statement. She believed it. There wasn't a flicker of doubt in her eyes. "You mean you heal with your touch?"

"With my touch, yes. The gift works when we make love. I'm a sexual healer."

He stared at her a long moment.

"You really believe that?" he had to ask, though a quiet voice inside him seemed to nod in satisfaction, as though this absurd statement somehow made sense. "And that's why all the men. You've healed them all…sexually?"

"It's okay if you don't believe me. It won't make any difference."

Again, the need to give to her overcame him. How

could he hurt her by telling her there was no such thing as sexual healing? A weariness filled him and he closed his eyes again. What did he know? Maybe she was right. "I don't know what to think."

"Then don't think." She smoothed her hand over his forehead, then kissed him. "Sleep. We need to be up early for the beach cleanup tomorrow."

He nodded, already drifting.

"Mason?"

A note of nervousness in her voice had him opening his eyes and reaching for her. "What is it, babe?"

"Will they like me? The teens?"

He kissed her hand, finally certain of something. "No doubt. They won't be able to resist your charm."

THE WIND PICKED UP and whipped sand across the bags of trash piled near a flagpole late the next afternoon. Tess dropped another bag on top of the rest and wiped her forehead as Mason moved beside her. She smiled, her heart quickening at the sparkle in his eye.

He had to be remembering their night together.

"I appreciate your coming to help," he said.

"No problem. I want to get involved. I think you're doing a good thing here." She nodded to a group of teens, laughing and playing as they made a game of gathering trash off the beach.

A quiver of nerves shot through her. They'd arrived a little late and the kids had already taken off up the beach with another volunteer. Mason hadn't yet had a chance to introduce her.

He shrugged. "We can only do so much. They came today. It's a good day."

"Well, my guess is that they have lots more good days than bad with Project Mentor around."

"We try to provide as many opportunities as we can. The youth center should have daily programs available. That will hopefully make more of a difference."

"Hey, Tess, Mason," Cassie called as she dumped a load of garbage, looking like one of the teens herself, with her hair pulled back in pigtails. Other members of the DCWC dotted the shoreline, working in pairs and groups mixed with the Project Mentor team.

"Look at that pile," she added, as she neared them. "It's a shame to see all this trash. You'd think people would care a little more."

Mason nodded. "At least this area will be clean for a while. We'll see what happens in another month or so. We might need to come back out."

"Mason, heads up." The young man from the park tossed a bag that flew past Mason's head, then landed in the pile.

He jogged up beside them. His gaze swept over the women, then away. He stopped with his hands on his knees.

"Rafe, this is Tess McClellan. Tess, Rafe Black."

Rafe nodded, his eyes cast to the ground. Tess extended her hand and the young man took it, his gaze skittering briefly to hers, before swerving away again. In the instant their eyes met a shock of feelings slammed into her: sorrow, pain, fear and a nearly debilitating sense of helplessness. She sucked in a deep breath and forced a smile, though the jumble of emotions raging through the young man had her knees wobbling. "It's nice to meet you, Rafe."

He ducked his head. "Yeah, it's nice to meet a friend of Dr. Davies. He's a good guy. He's helped me out a lot. Been there for me."

Mason gestured to Cassie. "This is Cassie Aikens. They're both with the Dade County Women's Club."

"Hi, Rafe." Cassie took his hand in both of hers and gave him a generous shake.

The boy bit his lip. "You're with the group that's raising money for the center?"

"That's right. Tess talked us into helping. I hear you and your friends want to pitch in." Cassie nodded toward the group of teens who straggled after Rafe, dragging bags with them.

"Uh, yeah." Rafe scuffed the toe of his shoe in the sand. "We thought since it was for the center..."

"We'd love to have your help," Cassie assured him. "Tess is going to coordinate your efforts. I've given her a list of jobs you kids can do."

Tess managed a smile for all the kids as their gazes turned to her. A jumble of feelings swamped her, much as they had with Rafe, but to varying degrees. She reached for Mason and he took her hand as he introduced the newcomers.

Her blood pounded in her ears and she bobbed her head mutely at each teen. So much for her empathic nature only working with her men. She needed to talk to Aunt Sophie about this new development. If she could shut the damn thing off, she would.

How could she bear the weight of all their emotions combined?

"You okay?" Mason squeezed her hand, concern rounding his eyes.

Strength seemed to flow into her from him and she gazed at him, awed. How did he manage it day in and day out with these kids—with his patients? A new respect for him flourished inside her.

"Tess?" he asked again.

She inhaled a deep breath and nodded. "It's great to meet all of you. I've really been looking forward to it."

"Rafe, how's your dad?" Mason asked.

The young man shifted and looked away. "About the same. I'm guessing it won't be long now." He shrugged. "I was going to ask you to help me declare my independence, but—" he shrugged again "—guess he needs me there for now."

His face brightened. "I went by to see that friend of yours at the car wash and he hired me on. Part-time, but that beats a blank and it's about all I can handle until I finish school."

Mason clapped him on the shoulder. "That's great to hear, Rafe. You have any trouble getting there?"

"It's on the bus line."

"So you go to school, work and help out your dad at home?" Cassie asked.

Rafe again ducked his head, uncertainty circling out from him. He seemed to be fighting an inclination to mistrust. "Yes, ma'am. Well—" he gestured to the rest of the teens who had gathered around a tall man, another of the Project Mentor volunteers "—we've got a little more to finish."

"It's looking good," Mason called as Rafe loped over to his friends.

"He seems like a great kid," Cassie said as she opened a new trash bag.

Tess tried to shake the intense turmoil that had gripped her since the moment Rafe had taken her hand. It was as if every ill feeling the young man—and his friends—had ever felt had clamored to escape through her. She mentally shook herself. "He's carrying around a lot of hurt."

Both Mason and Cassie turned to her, eyebrows raised in question. Her cheeks heated and she shrugged. "You can see it in his eyes."

Cassie nodded and waved as she left for a stretch of beach to their right. Mason handed Tess a fresh bag and they wandered toward a stand of sea oats clustered near the path leading back to the street where they'd parked.

They worked in silence for a while, Tess doing her best to release the upset the kids had stirred in her. She swallowed. She could barely tolerate a brief taste of what the boy had experienced.

How had he managed a lifetime?

"You are way too distracting," Mason said in an effort to lighten the mood as they picked up the last of the litter.

Had her unease been so apparent?

"I can't believe I nearly forgot about the beach cleanup this morning," he said.

She smiled and shifted her thoughts to safer territory, grateful he'd provided the opportunity. "I reminded you last night before we went to sleep."

"You made me late."

"I wanted you to start the day relaxed."

"Sweetheart, after last night I was nearly comatose. I'm not quite used to...ah...performing for such extended periods of time."

"I don't recall forcing you, not last night in the car, or on the coffee table in the living room, or against the wall in the hallway—"

"You got me started in the car. I'd never been quite so...experimental before. I couldn't seem to stop once we got started."

"You seemed experienced enough this morning. Even *I* have never had such an exciting shower. You *do* know how to work a showerhead." She forced a light tone.

"Okay, so you have this arousing effect on me. We'd better change the subject, or I'll have to drag you back to my place again."

Her blood warmed as her gaze met his and some of the unease left her. "I can't think of a better way to spend the rest of the day. That is, if you don't have anything else but your rounds scheduled. Is that right?"

He glanced up the beach to where Rafe and the rest of the teens moved slowly toward them, bags of trash in hand. "I need to see what's going on with the kids. We'll probably head out for pizza after this. I thought it would be a good time for you to get with them about the ball." He tossed her a sheepish glance. "So, what do you say? You up for pizza?"

Tess squelched the disappointment rising in her and stifled the discomfort that thinking of Rafe and the other teens brought her. How selfish could she be? Of course Mason had to spend time with the kids. But was she up to it? "You go ahead. I think maybe I'll pass today. I can get with them another time."

He stopped her with a hand on her arm. "Are you not feeling well? You look a little pale." He turned her to face him. "Babe, I'm so sorry. I should have let you get more rest last night. You didn't have to come. I could have taken you home. Here—" He started to drag her toward where they'd parked.

"No." She held her ground and he turned back to her. "I'm okay. I'm just not sure I can do this."

"What? Work with the kids?" His eyebrows arched in surprise. "They like you. You just need to give them a chance."

Her feeling of apprehension intensified. "I'm not sure what I can contribute to them, to be honest. I don't even know how to relate to them."

"You'll do fine. They need all the positive role models they can get. Tell you what, you don't need to meet with them today. We'll do that another time. Spend some time getting to know them." He cocked his head, his eyes coaxing. "It's just pizza."

"I don't know."

"Come for me, then. You don't have to talk to anyone else if you don't want to. Eat your pizza and keep me company."

"I don't want to intrude on your time with them."

"Don't be silly. You won't be intruding. Here, let's ask the kids." He nodded as the teens approached.

"No, Mason, don't." She tugged on her hand, trying to free herself from his grasp, but he held on tight.

"Hey, Rafe, don't you think that Tess should come for pizza?"

The young man's dark gaze glittered over her, and, though he shrugged and tried to look nonchalant, the hope in his eyes stopped her in her tracks. "That would be cool."

"See?" Mason turned to her. "How can you pass up an opportunity to be cool?"

She shook her head. "He didn't say *I'd* be cool if I went. He said *it* would be cool if I went. That's not the same thing at all."

"Same difference." Mason took her trash bag and heaved it onto the pile. "So, is it time for pizza, everyone?"

A cheer of accord rose from the group as the rest of the volunteers converged on the spot. Mason turned to Tess and extended his hand. "Ready?"

She glanced over the group of teens, some smiling, some sullen, some with a definite look of defiance. A different set of emotions radiated from each one. Everything about the teens seemed to be intensified tenfold compared to all the adults she'd ever dealt with.

No, she was anything but ready for this group. But her gut told her Mason needed her more than all of them combined, and if being with Mason meant weathering pizza with this crew, then pizza it was.

Lifting her chin, she placed her hand in his, her gaze intent on him. "As ready as I'll ever be."

"ARE YOU SURE YOU'LL be okay?" Mason cocked his head at Tess as he stood in her door, poised to leave later that evening.

Pizza with the Project Mentor teens had been as harrowing as Tess had feared. The strain of keeping a composed facade was taking its toll and she was grateful that he had to leave to do his rounds at the hospital.

She pressed a kiss to his cheek. "I'll be fine. You go do what you need to do."

"I can stop back by later." He wrapped one arm around her and pulled her close. "We can pick up where we left off this morning. There's all kinds of new places to try here." He glanced around the apartment. "You have some interesting nooks and crannies."

"And a sister who might pop in at any moment. Actually, I'm a little worn-out. Could I take a rain check?"

His disappointment reached out to her and she almost changed her mind, but weariness pressed on her and she smiled apologetically. "I guess you've just worn me out, Dr. Davies."

"Okay." He kissed the top of her head. "I'll let you off the hook for tonight. I'm on call tomorrow and I need to put some time in at the clinic downtown, so I'll call you when I can."

Her heart swelled with warmth for this man as he pulled her close and kissed her, his beautiful mouth telling her just how much he would miss her. She stood in the door as he moved down the hall, stopping to toss her a sexy smile before he turned onto the landing.

She sighed and leaned against the doorjamb for long moments after he'd gone. What to do with all these confusing new feelings? This relationship with Mason was getting more complicated all the time.

Taking a deep breath she locked and bolted the door, then stared at her quiet apartment. It was so strange to be here alone. When was the last time she'd been on her own on a Saturday night?

"This is as good a time as any to see if Erin wants to do something," she said to no one in particular as she punched in her sister's cell phone number.

Erin answered on the fourth ring, just when Tess was ready to hang up. "Erin McClellan here."

"Erin, hi. It's me, Tess." Tess shifted uneasily. She

hadn't spoken to her sister since their disagreement the other day. "So, it's Saturday night. Want to see a movie or something?"

A long silence buzzed across the line. "No, more to the left... I think I like the green one better, don't you? It picks up the stripe in the couch."

"Erin?"

"Sorry, Tess. Josh and I are trying to finish up the duplex this weekend, so we can start on the house for that neighbor of Nikki's next week."

"Oh, so you *are* working."

"Yeah... No, not you, Josh. Not that—yes, oh, that's good. What do you think?"

"I guess I'll let you go."

"Tess?"

"Yeah?"

"I know I said I'd make myself available, but I need to get this project finished. I am really swamped. You understand, don't you?"

"Oh, sure. No problem. I'll see what Nikki's up to tonight."

Erin laughed. "You're going to call her on a Saturday night? You don't think she and that hunky man of hers might be a little busy?"

"Yeah, I guess you're right. Well, I'll let you go. Tell Josh I said hello."

"Are you all right? You sound a little down or something."

"Just tired."

"Josh said to tell Mason hi for him. So how come Josh gets to meet him and not me?"

"Josh is working on the fund-raiser with us."

"Speaking of which, wasn't there something you wanted to ask me?"

"There was, but you're busy and then we got into that argument."

"So ask me."

"Josh already asked you, didn't he?"

"Maybe."

"So, do you want to or not?"

"Do I want to what or not?"

"Look, Erin, I am too tired for this. Do you want to do the decorations for the ball or not?"

"Josh says that everyone who's anyone will be there. That it'll be a great place to showcase my talents as a designer. Is that true?"

"It is if he has anything to do with it."

"Okay, I'm in."

"You are?"

"Yep."

"Just like that?"

"I said I'd do it. Now that Josh is helping me, I think I can manage it. It isn't like it will take the same kind of time the duplex or the house in Coral Gables will take. And it sounds like a great networking opportunity."

"It is."

"Then I'm on board. I'll even donate my services and provide everything else at cost, since it's for a good cause and all."

"Thanks, Erin, that's great. I really appreciate it. Mason and the DCWC will be thrilled. I'll give the decorating committee your number."

"Wait, Josh, don't. That's not straight. Look, Tess, I'm sorry to blow you off like this, but I've got to help him with these valances. Why don't you go ahead and give Nikki a call? She said we don't call her as much since she moved out and she misses that."

"She did?"

"Yeah, we had lunch yesterday."

"You did?" Envy flickered through Tess. "Why didn't you guys call me?"

"We did. You didn't pick up on your cell."

"I must have let the battery die again." She didn't mention that they could have called the nursery. For once she and Erin seemed to be having a civil conversation. Maybe she shouldn't push it.

"Okay, I'll see what Nikki's doing." She bid Erin goodbye, then punched Nikki's home number.

Nikki answered on the second ring. "Tess?"

"Hi, am I interrupting anything?"

"Like I'd answer the phone if you were."

"What's Dylan doing?"

"Watching football. I'm so glad you called. I thought about calling you, but I figured you'd be busy on a Saturday night, especially with a new guy to keep up with."

"Actually, I needed a little break. It's getting…I don't know…complicated."

"Why don't you come over? I'll mix up some margaritas and you can tell me all about it."

Tess sighed in relief. "I'm on my way."

11

An hour later Tess leaned toward Nikki, fingering her empty margarita glass. "So, what do you think? Have you lost the gift?"

Nikki drew a deep breath and relaxed against the cushions of her favorite oversize chair she'd brought into her new home. Here, in the recently renovated and decorated master bedroom, the chair seemed to fit better than it ever had in the apartment they'd shared.

Nikki shook her head. "Honestly, I'm not sure. I don't seem to attract men the way I used to. And I don't seem to *feel* things about people as much as I used to, either, though it almost seems that sense with Dylan has grown even stronger. I seem to feel everything he feels to an extreme degree. Do you know what I mean?"

To an extreme degree.

Tess nodded. Exactly the way she'd describe her experience with Mason. Just the way Aunt Sophie had theorized.

"Would it be such a bad thing? To lose the gift?" Nikki asked. "It was always more a curse than anything to me. Sure, it proved a blessing with Dylan. I honestly believe it helped him and I'm grateful for that, but I was barely aware that I had those abilities when I met him. It wasn't like I was very attached to them. I only accepted the gift once I believed it could help him."

She shuddered visibly. "I hate to think what would have happened if I hadn't met Dylan. The gift hasn't been nearly so kind to me as it's apparently been to you."

Tess frowned. "No regrets, then? About choosing Dylan over the gift—if indeed that's what's happened."

Pure happiness radiated from her sister, but even without her sixth sense Tess read Nikki's contentment in the blissful expression on her face.

"I'm happy for you, Nikki. Your engagement to Dylan seems to agree with you."

"It's a good life. You should think of trying it yourself. Find some nice guy to settle down with."

A shiver of foreboding swept over Tess. Settle down with a nice guy? Like Mason? "I can't imagine what that might be like. I don't even know if it's an option for me."

"I hear you're giving your minions a break. Or they're giving you one, however that works."

"It's weird. It has been strangely quiet around the apartment lately—when I've been there, that is. I guess I haven't been there much on the weekends. The break wasn't intentional. It seems that things just quieted down over the past week." She inhaled a breath. "Ever since I hooked up with Mason."

Did that have any significance?

"So tell me all about your new love. I hear he's knocked you for a loop."

"Who told you that? Erin? There she goes telling you things she has no idea about."

The corners of Nikki's lips lifted. "I don't know, that seems a pretty heated response."

"It is no such thing."

Nikki regarded her with raised brows.

"The only thing that I'm heated about is that little sister of ours talking about things that she doesn't know anything about."

"So he's not special? You weren't gushing? Erin said you were definitely gushing."

"Gushing? That's just a matter of opinion. Mason is...he's different. Special, yes. They've all been special, though, so it's hard to say. He cares about things the way most people don't. And these kids—I'm blown away by these kids he works with. He's just...amazing...and the patience he has. He sets his mind on something and— I don't know how I fit in. I feel things I'm not sure I want to feel, and I get all— Am I making any sense?"

"I've never seen you so flustered by a man."

"Who says I'm flustered? I am not flustered."

The phone on the side table rang. Tess started and Nikki frowned as she reached to answer it. "Hello?"

Tess folded her arms and sank back against the cushions of the chair Dylan had bought to match Nikki's. Tess was *not* flustered. So what if Mason was different from the rest? What did that have to do with anything? It certainly didn't mean she was planning to settle down with him—or anyone else for that matter.

"Wait, Thomas, say that again." Nikki plugged one ear and pressed the phone closer to her other ear.

Tess sat forward. Tension lined Nikki's face. A feeling of apprehension crept over Tess. Had something happened to Thomas? She cocked her head in question, but Nikki gestured for her to wait.

"Okay, well…I know… Just see if you can— I know… I know." She rolled her eyes and Tess relaxed some. Nikki was more frustrated than upset.

"Okay… Okay… We will. No, we will. Tess is here with me…. Yes, I hear." She flinched and pulled the phone away from her ear and a loud crashing sounded from the earpiece.

What was going on?

"Okay, Thomas, yes, we're coming…Yes, now. I promise. No, don't try to get in the middle of it. We're on our way." She glanced at Tess and raised her eyebrows in question.

"No way." Tess folded her arms and sat back. No way was she getting involved in whatever craziness Thomas had gotten himself into.

Nikki hung up the phone and stood. "Come on. I'm not doing this alone. You're coming with me."

"No, I'm not."

"Yes, you are. Maggie is much more likely to listen to you than to me."

"Maggie? I thought she was still hot-tubbing her way through Europe."

"Apparently, she got in last week."

"Last week?" Tess asked, stunned. "Why hasn't she called? Has she called you?"

Nikki's cheeks colored. "I don't know. Dylan took a break from his classes and we haven't been accessible."

Tess groaned but rose to follow her sister. "So where are we headed? What exactly is going on?"

"You don't want to know."

Tess groaned inwardly. "You're probably right, but tell me, anyway."

Only after grabbing her purse and ushering Tess out the garage door did Nikki answer. "Seems Maggie moved in with Aunt Sophie."

"What? What do you mean moved in?"

"Beats me. Something about she's tired of being on the road and it isn't like she has a place of her own to roost." Not a trace of derision laced Nikki's voice, a far cry from a few months ago.

"Okay, for just a minute let's say I buy that she's ready to roost. What is so wrong with her staying with Aunt Sophie? Doesn't she pretty much use that as a home base, anyway?"

Nikki shrugged as they reached the car. "Apparently this is different."

"How so?"

"It seemed Thomas was dodging pots and pans. He wasn't really up for any detailed explanations. One thing's for sure, though."

"What's that?"

"Maggie and Aunt Sophie are killing each other."

"WHAT THE HELL IS GOING on here?" Tess stared open-mouthed at Aunt Sophie's kitchen.

Dirt splattered the floor amid shards of broken pots and mangled herbs. A bowl of fruit lay on its side, its contents sprawled across the counter. Pots and pans littered the wooden floor.

She stared at first her mother, then Aunt Sophie, who sat at opposite ends of the long oak table. Thomas was nowhere to be seen. Nikki straightened the fruit bowl, then started to retrieve the contents.

"Well?" Tess asked again.

The two women sat in silence. Nikki waved a banana. "At least they've calmed down."

Tess shook her head. "Where's Thomas?"

Sophie gestured out the back door, which stood ajar. "As soon as the storm in here settled he stomped out back to light up his pipe."

"Aunt Sophie, I would expect this from Mom—" a derisive snort sounded from her mother's end of the table "—but I am shocked to witness this kind of behavior from you." She gestured to the disaster around them. "What is all this?"

Aunt Sophie's shoulders heaved. "Ask your mother."

Tess turned to Maggie, who waved her fingers in the air, then she pointed to Sophie. "She started it."

Sophie gasped but managed to hold her tongue. Tess pressed her palms to the table. "I don't care who started what. Why are the two of you fighting?"

Maggie rose, her red hair loose and wild-looking. "It doesn't matter. It's over and I'm leaving."

Sophie glared at her. "And where will you go?"

"Tess will take me in. Nikki's old room is still available, right girls?"

Tess shifted. "Not until you tell us what's been going on here."

"I'll tell you." Thomas spoke from the back door, his pipe in hand, smoke curling from the bowl. "They've lost their minds. That's what's happened."

"Just her." Maggie shook her finger at her sister. "My mind is fine. Maybe I should have known she'd be this way. I ask for one small, little favor and she can't handle it."

"One small, little favor?" Sophie's eyebrows arched and her face turned scarlet.

"What kind of favor?" Nikki asked as she finished filling the fruit bowl, then grabbed the broom and turned to the broken pots of herbs.

Sophie glared at Maggie and folded her arms. "You'll have to ask her."

"It isn't anything any *loving* sister wouldn't do for another."

"Now, Maggie." Thomas went to her and gripped her shoulders. "Sophie loves you. Whatever the two of you are in a tizzy about, there's one thing for sure. The two of you do love each other and you'll work this out."

Maggie shook her head. "I should never have come here." One large tear rolled down her cheek. "It was a huge mistake. I thought for sure she'd understand."

She turned to Tess. "Look, I am really tired. Can I come stay with you or not?" She raised her arms, then let them flop to her sides. "Otherwise, I'll go find a hotel."

"No." Sophie rose, then moved to her sister's side. Thomas draped one arm protectively around Maggie's shoulders and pulled her close. A sound of frustration rose in Sophie's throat. "You'll stay here."

"No." Maggie lifted her chin. "Not unless you agree to my terms."

Sophie shook her head. "We need to discuss this rationally. And right now, you are not rational."

"No discussion. I'm not the one being irrational." Maggie turned to Tess. "Yes or no, Tess?"

"No," Sophie repeated. "You'll stay here. I'll grant your favor."

Maggie's shoulders slumped as though she'd been relieved of some great burden. "Thank you, Sophie. You won't be sorry. I promise."

"I'd better not be." Sophie's voice shook and a feeling of unease settled over Tess.

In her entire life she had never seen her aunt anything but calm and serene. What could possibly have happened to throw her so off kilter?

Try as she might, she couldn't seem to *read* either her mother or her aunt. Not that she ever had, but given today's development, it had been worth a try. She turned to Thomas. He scratched his head, seemingly as confused as the rest of them.

"If it's okay with all of you, I'm going to bed." Dark rings circled Maggie's eyes and she did indeed appear ready to collapse.

"No, it's not okay." Tess frowned first at her mother, then her aunt. "We deserve an explanation."

Shaking her head, Sophie glared at Maggie, who ran her hand over her face, then turned toward them. "You're right. You deserve an explanation, but for now you're not getting one. I will decide when to tell you anything."

"Wait," Nikki said. "You two have some secret and you're just not going to tell us?"

"That's what makes it a secret, dear." Maggie moved toward the stairs. "Good night, all. I really do need to get some rest."

"Here, I'll walk you up," Thomas offered, and she nodded, leaning into him as they moved up the first step.

After they'd gone, Tess turned to Sophie, but before she could utter a word, Sophie raised her hand to silence her. "This is between your mother and me. It's the way she wants it, so it's the way it's going to be. At least for now."

"Aunt Sophie..." Nikki set down the broom to move to Sophie's side. "You know if there's anything either of you need from us, all you have to do is ask."

"I know, sweet girl." Sophie cupped Nikki's cheek, then gestured to Tess. "Come here, both of you. Your old aunt needs a hug after all this drama."

Tess complied and Sophie wrapped her arms around them both. For just a second a flicker of fear passed through Tess. She straightened, but the sensation was gone so quickly, she couldn't tell if she had imagined it, or exactly where it had come from.

Had she gotten a reading from her aunt?

"Now, you both run along. I'm sorry you got dragged into this. Poor Thomas didn't know what else to do but call in the troops when he walked in on us."

Tess caught her aunt's eye. "Are you sure the two of you will be okay?"

"Of course." Sophie straightened and smoothed her cotton dress. "Aren't we always?"

"*You* certainly are." Nikki leaned in to kiss her on the cheek. "Mom looked exhausted. Is she okay?"

A shadow flickered across Sophie's eyes, but again passed so quickly that Tess wasn't sure it had actually been there. The reading from her own gut had her shifting uncomfortably.

"It's good to hear you call her that. She'll be fine." Sophie smiled, though it seemed forced. "She just needs a little rest. It seems it's taking her a little longer to get over her jet lag this time, but she'll be fine." Her smile brightened, seeming even more unnatural. "I'll look after her. There's absolutely nothing for you two to worry your pretty heads about."

"Okay, then, if you're sure, we'll get going." Nikki nodded to Tess.

Tess kissed her aunt's cheek. "You call if you need us, okay?"

"We'll be fine, dear. Remember, Thomas is a shout away if we need him. Bless him for moving into the neighborhood, where we can see him more regularly."

Tess nodded, then followed Nikki out the door. They walked in silence to the car, and drove a mile or more before Nikki turned to her, her hands gripping the wheel. "Did I imagine it, or did you feel it, too?"

The sense of unease twisted Tess's stomach. "Did I feel what?"

Nikki turned back to the road and shrugged, though her grip on the wheel didn't loosen. "You know, that sense of mine isn't working anymore the same way it used to. I probably imagined it."

Tess kept her gaze on the road. A streetlight flashed by. "Imagined what?"

"I don't know. For just a second there— It's probably nothing, but I thought that maybe I sensed this flicker of fear from Aunt Sophie." She glanced at Tess. "Did you get any of that?"

Tess shifted. "What would Sophie be afraid of? I've never known that woman to back down from anything."

"Exactly. Which is the only reason I brought it up." She shook her head, then continued to speak. "I hate that they're keeping this secret from us. It so obviously has her spooked. Whatever it is, it has something to do with Maggie. There's something terribly wrong with her."

The knot in Tess's gut tightened. She sighed. "Yes, I think you're probably right. I got the exact same feeling. Something is definitely wrong with Mom. The question is, what can we do about it? She obviously doesn't want us to know."

"Damn, Tess. You were supposed to tell me I was hallucinating."

She met Nikki's gaze. "If you were, then I was right there with you."

"SO WHAT COULD IT BE?" Tess paced across Mason's soft carpet, while he waited patiently for her to join him in his bed the next evening.

"Sweetheart, there's no way for me to tell."

"But you're a doctor. Tell me some signs to look for. She seemed really tired. There were dark rings under her eyes. You know, or maybe you don't know, but she has always looked years younger than her actual age. People have been mistaking us for sisters since Nikki and I hit our teens, but Maggie was starting to look her age last night. What could possibly do that to a person?"

"Tess, come to bed. You're getting yourself all worked up and you don't know that anything is really wrong. Maybe she was just feeling jet lag, like your aunt said."

"Oh, no, there's definitely something wrong. She and Aunt Sophie never argue like that. And this was no ordinary argument. This was an all-out fight. They demolished the kitchen. I've never seen anything like that, except for the time at the apartment when the guys got a little carried away over that football game and Josh took a pass in the kitchen and they all had to get in on the action.

"But that's beside the point. Nikki picked up on it, too. Sophie is helping Maggie hide it, but whatever it is is *not* good."

"Come." He patted the bed. "You need to relax. If you really want to help your mother, you should calm down so you can think clearly."

Tess sighed as she crawled into the bed beside him. "I guess you're right. I just don't know how to react to this. Do you know that I can't ever remember her having so much as the sniffles?"

"Good, she's generally healthy, then. Is there any family history of illness?"

"No, but I don't have what you would call a normal family. I can't tell you much about my grandfather's side, but my grandmother comes from unusually strong stock. All the women of my family tend to live relatively long and healthy lives. I think my great-aunt Emma was one hundred and three when she went peacefully in her sleep."

"That's good."

She turned to him, her eyebrows drawn down in concern. "So how do I figure out what's up with my mother?"

"Well, you can always ask her."

"I did. She was adamant that she wouldn't tell."

He stroked his hand up her back. "What about your aunt? Could you ask her?"

"She made it pretty clear that it was between my mother and her. I don't think she'll break that confidence." She sighed again and rested her head on his chest. "I hate this. I'm thinking all kinds of horrible things here. I just can't imagine what it could be."

"Maybe you should try to put it aside and not think about it. If it's anything serious, then chances are she'll broach the subject when she's ready."

"But what if you saw her? Checked her out kind of discreetly."

His hand stilled on her back. He shifted to see her better. "What are you saying?"

"I could arrange a dinner. My sisters both want to meet you and some of my other friends, too, so maybe I could have a cookout at my place and you could come and I could invite Mom and the rest and you could make some objective observations about whatever doctorly things you would normally observe in a patient and—"

"Tess, I know that you're worried, but I simply can't do that."

"Well, why not? You don't have to examine her per se, just give me your opinion on how she seems."

"First of all, without a proper examination and thorough questioning, I doubt I could tell you any more than you already know. Second, as a doctor I live by a certain code of ethics and this falls way beyond the area I operate in. Lastly, even if it didn't, there are all kinds of laws that protect a person's health information. I could get into trouble on several levels."

Disappointment weighed down on her. "So what am I supposed to do?"

He resumed stroking her back. "The best you can do

is not worry until you know you have something to worry about."

"Yeah, right." She snuggled in closer to him and yawned. Maybe she was actually tired enough to finally get some sleep. She'd hardly been able to shut her eyes last night. "That'll be easier said than done."

He was silent a long moment and she was just starting to drift off when he said, "You know, I'd like to meet your family and your friends, even if they're like the rest of the friends I've met—of the male persuasion. I'm sure I'd get all kinds of insights."

"I'm sure you would." She frowned.

Without a possible diagnosis for whatever might be ailing her mother as an outcome, her cookout plan had lost some of its appeal. The idea of Mason in the same room with her guys, not to mention her family, didn't quite sit right with Tess for some reason.

"So, when do you want to do it?" he asked.

"Do what?"

"The cookout."

"I don't want to take up all your time off. We have so much to do to get ready for the ball and only a few more weeks to do it. I don't know how we'll get it all finished in time. Most of the marketing is done, but we have to get the programs to the printer's. I should get with the teens. Cassie says the hotel wants us all to come in to sample appetizers, and we still have to decide on a band, and there's all those last-minute details—"

"We can take time for this. It's important. I really want to meet your family. Tell you what. I'll make it easy on you. I'll bring the steaks. How about Saturday?"

"Like in a week? That Saturday?"

"Yep. A week from yesterday, in the afternoon. I'm taking Rafe to the game that night, but I can be there the whole day with you."

Her gut screamed at her to make up an excuse, any excuse, but the enthusiasm in Mason's quiet words called to her in a way she could hardly resist. So he wanted to meet her family. What harm could come from that?

She leaned up to look at him, and the hope in his eyes would have convinced her if she hadn't already made up her mind. "Okay, Saturday afternoon. My place. I'll have the whole crew there."

12

SMOKE CURLED FROM THE gas grill on Tess's deck. Mason breathed deeply the scent of grilling chicken and steaks and did his best to relax. Why was he getting all tense? This was a simple cookout.

He'd asked for it himself. With all Tess was doing to help his teens—the closest thing to family he had—he felt obliged to run the gauntlet with her family. If they were anything like Tess, he was bound to love them.

And as far as all her male companions...well, best to have a clear idea of what he was up against. Seeing her interact with them here in her home should give him an idea of whether or not he had anything to worry about.

"Penny for your thoughts?" He slipped an arm around the object of his obsession and nuzzled her ear as she fussed over the grill. The apartment had already been teeming with people by the time he'd arrived. When Tess had slipped out he'd followed her to steal this moment alone.

She leaned into him. "Oh, just wondering if there's enough food."

Mason laughed. "There are casseroles, side dishes and desserts in there. Your friend Ramon is still busy in the kitchen, and it seems every one of your relatives brought a truckload of food. It's going to take an army to finish it all off as it is."

"I don't know. We McClellans tend to have rather robust appetites."

"Yeah, I remember, but I think your eyes are bigger than your stomach." He rubbed his hand across her flat belly for good measure. "I don't know where you put it all. I think you just like to order large."

"We cook like we order."

"Either way, you've got plenty of food."

So something else was bothering her. Was she still worried about her mother, or was it the teens? Or could it be she was as tense as he was about him meeting her people?

The sliding door opened, spilling assorted houseguests onto the deck. Tess's sister, Nikki, whom he'd just met, greeted them with a smile, her brown eyes warm with what seemed genuine welcome. "There they are."

"Mmm, smells great." Max, whom Nikki had introduced as one of Tess's *minions,* lifted the lid on the grill. "Hey, want me to flip these?"

"Thanks." Tess handed him the tongs as Nikki and their aunt Sophie closed in on Mason.

A bolt of apprehension raced through him, then Tess's aunt winked and the worry seemed to drain from him.

"Hey, everyone, let's go back inside and see what the rest of them are doing." Tess moved beside him, taking his arm in an endearingly protective gesture. "Has Erin gotten back yet? She said she'd work just half a day today, so she could join us."

Sophie waved her aside. "She called to say she's on her way. And we are *not* going back inside just yet. It's finally cool enough out to draw a decent breath, and for once there's a bit of a breeze. We're sitting right here for now. Isn't that right, Mason?" She gave him a measured look and motioned him into one of the wrought-iron chairs at the table.

Mason drew himself up tall and favored Sophie with his best smile as he held a chair first for her, then for Nikki. "Yes ma'am, it's not bad out here at all."

Tess didn't wait for an invitation. She scooted into the seat beside him, before he could pull out her chair. If Sophie meant to question Mason, it seemed Tess meant to stay beside him. He took her hand and squeezed it to reassure her. He got the feeling from her aunt that she'd already taken his measure and he'd passed.

Tess held on and he tossed her a sideways glance. She *was* nervous about this. Did her fretting over whether or not he'd cut it with her family have anything to do with her own reaction to the Project Mentor kids? He straightened as that now-familiar feeling of warmth expanded his chest.

Whatever apprehensions she had over working with the teens, he planned to stick by her side through it.

"Tess, dear, why don't you get us all something cold to drink?" Sophie smiled sweetly at her.

Tess opened her mouth to protest, but Mason gave her hand another squeeze. "I could use a beer, if you have one."

"Oh, me, too," Nikki said. "Would you mind?"

"Make that three," Sophie instructed. "And please send that mother of yours out here. How can we have a proper interrogation without her?"

Nikki laughed, but Tess's eyes rounded. "Aunt Sophie, you can't. That isn't why I invited all of you."

"Of course it is. We've never had a big cookout for any of your other minions—"

"I hate that word." Tess stood and clenched her fists. "If one more person calls them that—"

"Settle down, dear. We mean Mason no harm. He obviously isn't like the others, which is why we need to determine exactly what is going on here."

Tess stood tense and livid for a moment, seemingly too overcome to speak. Mason patted the back of her thigh. So, he was different from the rest? Somehow, that knowledge gave him a boost, had him sitting taller in his seat.

"It's okay, babe. You go on in and send out your mother. I'm sure it will all be okay. Nikki will protect me if things get out of hand." He grinned at Nikki and she smiled at him, her eyes sparkling.

"That's right, Tess. You can't be objective here,' Nikki said. "That's why you need us. I'll report everything. I promise."

"No." Tess stomped her foot and remained at Mason's side. "This is intolerable. I will not allow you to perform some kind of interrogation in my own home. It's uncalled-for. Not to mention completely humiliating."

Max waved the tongs from his spot by the grill. "Hey, Ramon and I can sit in, if you want a full panel, Sophie."

"What?" Tess stared at him, her mouth gaping. "Max, how could you turn on me like this?"

"Your aunt has a point. You just haven't been yourself lately." His gaze moved to Sophie. "Should I get Ramon?"

"Oh, no, dear—"

"Well, thank you." Tess looked with relief at her aunt, her shoulders relaxing.

"Ramon is making those little crab cakes I love. Could you see if one of the others is available? Thomas is busy helping Ramon, but how about Todd? Is he still here?"

"What?" Tess's face took on a bright hue.

Sophie rose and touched Tess's arm. "You go in with Max. We'll be in shortly. Don't you worry about a thing. I promise we won't hurt him." She handed Tess over to Max. "Now, have Ramon keep her busy. And don't forget to bring Maggie and Todd when you return."

"And the beer," Nikki reminded.

"Yes, beer for everyone." Sophie gestured to the group at the table. "Unless you'd like something a little stiffer, Mason?"

"Ah, no, thanks, a beer will be just fine. I have a feeling I'd better keep my wits about me."

"Good choice." Sophie turned back to Tess. "See, he's doing great already. Smart man."

As Max escorted her inside, Tess threw Mason a glance that said she was sorry and mortified and wished him luck all at once. Then he was alone with her sister and her aunt and not even a beer to fortify him. Still, as he glanced at her aunt she again winked reassuringly.

He relaxed and smiled at the two. "So, Nikki, I hear you're marrying an architect."

She tilted her head. "He's not quite an architect yet, but he's working on it. You'll get to meet him. He's just gone for ice."

"Dylan was a lawyer when my niece met him, but he was not a very happy lawyer. You're a doctor, aren't you?" Sophie regarded him with raised eyebrows, her interest seemingly genuine.

"I'm an internist. I have a practice in Pembroke Pines."

"And that free clinic in downtown Miami, right?" Nikki asked.

"I helped to found it with a number of colleagues. I volunteer one day a week down there and take a night on call."

"And you're happy with your work?" Sophie turned and smiled as Max returned with a newcomer Mason hadn't yet met, but who, with her flaming waves, could be no other than Tess's mother.

"Where's Todd and the beer?" Sophie waved them toward the table. "Oh, there he is. Come on, everyone. Todd, drop those beers and get a couple of chairs from inside."

She helped pass out the drinks, while Todd dragged out a couple of heavy chairs from the kitchen. He shook his head as he sat. "Tess is fit to be tied. I'm not sure if Ramon and Thomas can handle her."

"Maybe I should check on her." Mason pushed back his chair.

"Oh, no you don't, young man. We haven't been properly introduced." Tess's mother smiled at him from across the table, her eyes the same blue as her daughter's, though they somehow lacked the luster that shone in Tess's.

"Maggie McClellan, Dr. Mason Davies." Sophie made the introductions.

Maggie offered her hand and Mason took it, noting that her fingers were icy to the touch. He mentally filed away the information. He had no intention of assessing her the way Tess had asked, yet he couldn't help but note that she did look rather tired. Not that it detracted from her beauty.

Mason settled again, as he faced what, indeed, seemed a panel of Tess's friends and family ready to interrogate him. It dawned on him that he very much wanted to make a good impression.

Sophie clasped her hands on the table. "Mason was just telling us whether or not he's happy in his work as an internist."

He nodded. "Yes, actually, I'm quite satisfied in my work."

"What is it that you like about it?" Maggie asked.

"Well, medicine isn't an exact science, but there are certain procedures and precedents one can count on. I like that when a patient comes to me I have a protocol to call on to determine what might be the cause of his or her complaint."

"So you like the order of the medical world?" Todd narrowed his eyes. "That's interesting. It's like he's almost an opposite to Tess."

Several heads nodded in agreement, and Mason fisted his hand around the beer bottle. Did he sound like some heartless baboon they wouldn't want Tess involved with? "It isn't just the order. I like the people. I meet people from all walks of life at my practice and particularly at the free clinic. I've met some amazing kids through Project Mentor. They've taken my life in a direction I hadn't anticipated."

"Kids?" Maggie's eyebrows rose. "Did you just say that you work with children?"

"Yes, some children. Mostly teens." He shrugged, not sure how to sum up the nonprofit work. "We're helping them to find their way."

Max crossed his arms and leaned back in his chair. "And Tess is getting involved with this?"

"She's organizing the teens to help with the fundraiser and she participated in a beach cleanup with them."

"Wait a minute." Nikki frowned. "Tess was at the beach and she picked up trash—with kids?"

"That's right."

A grin burst across Nikki's face. "Unbelievable. I would have liked to have seen that."

Sophie gazed at him with her keen gray eyes. "Mason, you do realize that this is all rather unprecedented for my niece?"

"No. I'm sorry, I don't follow."

"Tess's normal outing to the beach usually includes an entourage of guys—" Nikki gestured toward Max and Todd "—carrying her cooler, setting up her umbrella, then entertaining her with antics."

"Well, sort of." Max shifted in his seat. "But we always have a good time."

"Yeah." Todd nodded. "Tess has a big heart and she's lots of fun, but it's hard to picture her hanging with a bunch of kids." He turned to Max. "So she's dumped us to hang with this guy and help the community."

"Really can't argue with that." Max turned to the rest. "Maybe Sophie is right. Tess hasn't been herself lately, but that isn't necessarily a bad thing."

"No, not at all." Sophie's eyes shone. "She has this rather enchanting glow about her, especially when she's with you."

"Really?" Mason smiled, that warm feeling spreading through him. "You think I make her glow?"

"Oh, definitely," Max said, and murmurs of assent rounded the table.

Tess's mother leaned toward him. "It was the same with Nikki when she met Dylan."

Nikki nodded. "And she does nothing but gush about you."

"Gush?" he asked.

"Yes, gush. She can't say enough good about you."

"And glows," Todd added.

"Gushes and glows?" Mason lifted his beer, smiling. For an interrogation, this seemed to be going quite well.

More nods and murmurs of assent.

"It's very un-Tess-like behavior." Sophie took a thoughtful sip. "And look how she defended you just now. You're obviously very important to her."

"I hope so. She means a lot to me," Mason said slowly, and set down his beer.

"Of course she does." Max shrugged, while Sophie cocked her head and assessed him with a new intensity.

"What exactly does that mean—that she means a lot to you?" she asked, and the others looked at her questioningly, before turning to Mason.

His gut tightened and he took another swig from his beer. What had happened to all the talk of gushing and glowing? He had the distinct impression that he was missing something important. "It means that I've really come to care for her. I care a lot for her. I want her to be happy, just like the rest of you do."

Max screwed up his face as though he was trying hard to understand something. "You *care* for her?"

"What's with that?" Todd asked.

Mason blinked at him. What was he supposed to say? That he *didn't* care for her? "I'm sorry, I'm not sure I understand what you're all getting at."

"He can't say it, can he?" Max's eyes rounded, the whites of his eyes showing.

Mason squirmed, the seat of the chair suddenly harder than he'd realized. "Can't say what?"

"Don't you see?" Sophie smiled as though she'd figured something out. "He's in denial."

Maggie nodded and Nikki pursed her lips. "So that's his thing, that he's kind of closed himself off?"

"It's a defense mechanism of sorts, I think." Maggie cocked her head and Mason had that feeling of being observed through a magnifying glass.

"Hey, you don't have to talk around me like I'm not here," he said, unable to resist the urge to defend himself. "Whatever you have to say, you can just come out and say it. I can take criticism."

"No criticism, dear," Sophie said. "Just an observation. I find all this quite fascinating."

"Yes," Maggie added. "It's as if they're breaking all the rules. What with the way Nikki has stayed with Dylan."

"I'm very law-abiding, I assure you."

"Of course you are." Sophie smiled at him. "I'll bet you follow all the rules."

"I certainly do. I pride myself on always doing my best to do the right thing."

"You colored inside all the lines as a child, follow standard safety rules, vote and floss on a regular basis." Tess's mother gestured matter-of-factly with both hands as she spoke.

He drew a deep breath, feeling a little more on steady ground. "That's right."

"So he really can't say it? He has repression issues?" Max nodded. "Just like Todd here had a stutter and Evan couldn't stand to be in small places and I had those allergies."

"What does all that have to do with anything?" Mason stared at the man, trying desperately to grasp whatever he was missing in the conversation.

"He's saying that you all have a reason for being with my niece and that your reason is your inability to express emotion." She squinted at him. "Though I think that's more a symptom hiding a deeper issue."

Mason straightened. "I express emotion."

"But you can't say it. Has anyone not been able to say it before?" Todd asked Nikki.

She laughed. "It used to make me roll my eyes with all the emoting that usually goes on around here."

"What?" Mason spread his hands in appeal. "I can emote. What is it that I'm supposed to say? I'll say it. Just tell me what it is."

"Dude." Todd smiled. "It's easy. You feel for Tess what we've all felt for her in varying degrees. What we still feel for her, though it's mellowed in a sense. Max and I know because we've both been there."

"It's nothing to be afraid of," Max continued for him. "It really isn't anything you can help. It's out of your control. It's bigger than you."

"What?" Mason couldn't keep the frustration from his voice as a bead of sweat rolled down his cheek. "What is out of my control?"

"You might as well just admit it, bro. Like Max said,

it's out of your control. Tess has this thing about her that it's just pointless to resist." Todd shook his head. "I'm amazed that you've managed to fight it for this long."

At the knowing looks around the table, it was all Mason could do to stay in his seat. He took a deep breath and faced them, as though he were facing the world's toughest firing squad. As calmly as he could, he returned Sophie's piercing gaze. "Okay, give it to me straight, because I can't make sense of any of this."

Her gray eyes softened. "It's simple, Mason. You're in love with Tess, dear."

MASON SHIFTED ON THE bleachers that evening and went through the motions of cheering as the Hurricanes scored and Rafe went wild along with the crowd around him. Mason forced himself to focus on the game.

This was Rafe's night of football, hot dogs and time away from his old man. The boy deserved it. By all indications he was working his butt off to make something of his life. Mason really meant to be there for the young man, but memories from the cookout just wouldn't leave him alone.

You're in love with Tess, dear.

Sophie's words rang through his mind. He'd never been so stunned as when she'd uttered them. Of course he cared for Tess…but love? That was a huge leap. And what had they meant about his repressing his emotions?

Yet his gut tightened the more he dwelled on the conversation. So what was wrong with coloring inside the lines? He'd always taken pride in his work. What were they all saying about his need to conform?

He didn't always conform. Hadn't he recently been

swimming with all his clothes on? The other day he'd ordered two entrées, much to Tess's approval. And what about all the incredible sex he and Tess had been having? Certainly Uncle Al would have frowned at their blatant disregard for convention there.

Not that Mason cared what Uncle Al thought. The man was alone and bitter, a shell of the man he could have been. Mason was *not* following in his uncle's footsteps.

"Hey, are we going or what?"

Startled, Mason glanced up at Rafe. The crowd was dispersing along the bleachers. Apparently the game had ended. "Oh, sure."

"We won, by the way. That was what all that yelling was about."

Mason nodded as they shuffled out behind an older couple dressed in matching Hurricanes T-shirts and caps. "I'm sorry, Rafe. Guess I've been a little distracted."

"What's up? Trouble with your lady?"

"No, not really." Tess had been so embarrassed by her family's interrogation she'd bent over backward to make amends the rest of the afternoon. "She's been great."

"She sure is fly."

Mason nodded. She was more than that. Tess was everything he could ever want in a woman. Meeting her had been an unexpected boon. The last thing he'd wanted was to jump into another relationship, but how was he supposed to resist something as unexpected as…Christmas in July?

"You've changed since you met her."

He glanced at Rafe as they exited the stadium and made their way toward the parking garage. "I have?"

"You used to be more uptight about stuff—like reserved or something. But you've loosened up a lot."

"Yeah, maybe I have." He shook his head, suddenly chagrined.

Of course he'd loosened up. Tess had done that for him. Before he'd met her he'd never swum in the Atlantic with all his clothes on, or ordered anything unusual off a menu, and he'd certainly never made love in his car, on the coffee table and against a wall all in one night before.

He was a new man because of her. What was it Sophie had said? Something about his being with Tess for a reason. Was this why he was with her, to help him learn how to color outside of the lines?

"Who gets chicks anyway? They're like a big mystery. I don't know why we even bother. We're not ever going to figure them out."

"You may be right, Rafe, but we owe it to ourselves to give it our best shot."

Rafe grinned. "So you giving it your best shot with Ms. Tess?"

"I don't think I really have been, but I'm going to change that." Excitement poured through him as a plan formed in his head. He needed to try something bold and daring to show her how he felt.

"Yeah? What're you going to do?"

He smiled at Rafe as they reached his car. "I'm going to color outside of the lines."

13

TESS INHALED A SHARP BREATH and expectation filled her as Mason led her into the arcade where she'd taken him the day she'd tried to teach him how to be spontaneous. "Mason, I'm so excited that you wanted to come here. I didn't think you'd ever come back."

He smiled. A sense of satisfaction flowed outward from him. "Someone suggested that I needed to learn how to color outside of the lines. I thought this might be the place to get started."

"Oh, look." She clapped her hands and ran to what appeared to be some type of rowing machine. "Let's do this. It's a blast."

Lights flashed across the top of the machine as a screen depicted a digital couple shooting rapids and narrowly missing boulders and waterfalls.

Mason eyed the double seat and paddles and seemed to struggle with his immediate inclination to leave. "Wouldn't you rather rent a real boat somewhere and paddle to your heart's content?"

"Sure, we'll do that sometime. But we're here and this is fun." She scrambled up into one of the seats. Turning, she gestured for him to join her. "Come on. You're going to love it."

He took a deep breath and nodded. "You're right. I'm up for this."

A smile curved her lips and she patted the seat beside her. "Okay, we'll work together then, as a team."

He inserted his game card into the slot, then searched for a start button.

"Here." Tess leaned across him.

His fresh scent surrounded her as the warmth of his body melted into her. An intoxicating mixture of serenity and excitement shot through her. She floated for a moment, caught up in a feeling of well-being. Then the seat bucked beneath them.

"Row." Tess laughed and pulled on the oar beside her, while trying to shift her focus from Mason to the game.

Water rushed toward them on the screen, the roar of the current and tilting of their boat oddly realistic.

"Row!" she said again, her voice kicking up a notch as a boulder loomed before their animated counterparts.

Mason pulled hard on his oar and the picture spun in a dizzying circle. Blood pumping, Tess cried out and threw herself against him, leaning on her oar. "We have to pull out of this spin—watch out!"

Somehow they managed to straighten their course. For a few exhilarating moments they rode the rapids, completely in control, their movements synchronized as they averted various obstacles. Tess's blood rushed through her veins. "Left! Now right!"

The counter on the screen zeroed out and the game ended. Mason's excitement curled around both of them. He dropped his oar. "No way."

Again, Tess laughed. "See, I knew you'd like it. I told you that you should always listen to me."

"Maybe." He grinned. "But we didn't even get close to the finish line."

"We did okay. We had a good run. Winning isn't everything, Mason."

"It is where I come from."

Her heart twisted and she reached for him. "I'm sorry to hear that, babe."

For a moment he leaned in toward her, but then he pushed away and climbed from the seat. "Let's go find something I know I can win."

Tess stared at him in wonder as she trailed after him. He looked like a normal man. Sure, he was good-looking, but he had no extraordinary characteristics that might account for the unusual effect he had on her. Just as Nikki had said it was with her and Dylan, it was as though Mason's mere presence intensified her senses, her every emotion and nuance of feeling.

Gloom settled over her. How was she to move on once their loving was over?

He looked up from his intent perusal of a pinball machine. "I think I can do this."

She smiled in spite of herself. "Of course you can. It's pinball."

"Yeah?" He moved aside and gestured for her to step up to the game. "Let's see you do it."

She folded her arms, her sullen mood returning. "I don't feel like it."

"No way. If I'm going to play, so are you."

With a shake of her head she stepped up to the game, pulled back the control to launch the pinball, then let it fly. Lights flashed across the display and bells dinged as the ball made a feeble pass through the playing field.

"No, no, no. It's in the wrist." Mason shooed her aside, then with a great show he sent the next ball flying. The machine lit up and the bells rang incessantly, adding up his score as the ball hit nearly every target.

He turned, a triumphant grin plastered across his face. "Now that—" he gestured broadly to his winning score "—is how you play pinball."

Unable to control her growing irritation, Tess glared at him. "It's just a game, Mason. A silly game."

His eyes rounded. "What's wrong? I thought you were up for a little fun. I thought you'd be happy to see me letting free my inner child."

She stared at him a long moment. Was that what was wrong? This new playful Mason was a healing—if not healed—Mason. He no longer seemed to bear the conservative yoke that had been so evident when they'd first met. Was this new playfulness a sign that he'd soon be out of her life?

"I don't want to talk about it. I'm hungry," she said, changing the subject. "Let's get something to eat."

"Okay, but hold on a minute." He ran to the ticket counter and plopped down his small stack of tickets he'd pulled from the pinball machine. "I would like one of those, please," he said to the acne-faced attendant, pointing to a grouping of colored plastic rings.

The young man pulled out a basket of the rings and set it on the counter. "Which one?"

Mason turned to Tess. "Your choice."

She regarded him with raised eyebrows.

"It's for you."

Sighing, she looked over the assortment. A small

part of her perked up at the prospect that he'd won the ring for her. "The blue one."

"Good choice." Mason picked out the ring, then turned and held it out to her, his expression solemn. "Tess McClellan, will you wear this ring as a symbol of the depth of my affection for you and to seal our commitment to this relationship?"

Startled, she stared at the ring and chose her words carefully. "Mason, you know I'm committed to this relationship for as long as it may last."

He nodded, then slipped the ring on her finger. "Then we should make the most of it." He gripped her hand and his gaze pinned her. "Move in with me, Tess. Live with me and share my life."

She blinked at him for what must have been a full minute before she pulled back her hand. "Mason, exactly what are you saying?"

He shrugged. "Live with me."

"I heard that part. I'm just having a little trouble absorbing it."

"What's so hard to absorb? Look how well we've been getting along." He gripped her arms. "Do you know how hard that is to find—how rare it is?"

"Yes, but…" He was right. As many relationships as she'd had, she'd never before experienced the kind of rapport she and Mason shared.

"But what, Tess? You're always telling me not to hold back, but here you are, holding back."

"No, it's not that."

He folded his arms and waited for her to continue.

Like she did so often with him, she searched for the right words. She glanced at the young man behind the counter, then moved with Mason toward the exit. "I know you didn't really believe me when we talked about my gift."

He stared at her, his expression blank.

"Let's sit." As they exited the building, she glanced around for a shaded place. She led him to a short bench in a nearby covered breezeway.

He settled beside her. "Look, Tess, I know this is a big step. It scares the hell out of me, too."

"Yes, but listen first. There's something I need to explain."

He leaned forward, his gaze intent. "Okay, I'm listening. You want to talk about...your gift."

"Yes, my gift of sexual healing. I need you to take me seriously."

A horn honked in the distance. A small group exited a nearby restaurant, chatting quietly. His frown deepened. "Babe, I wouldn't have asked you to live with me if I wasn't taking you seriously. But sexual healing?"

Confusion and doubt spun out from him, but below that a part of him believed her, though he seemed inclined to suppress it. "See, part of the gift is that I'm empathic. I can tell that you're finding it hard to believe what I'm saying, even though there's a part of you, deep down, that knows it's true."

"That's pretty standard. Just about anyone could have guessed that."

"You don't want to believe it, but you can't dispute the fact that something unusual, something maybe even magical happens when we're together."

"You're telling me that this sexual healing is real? That this is your gift?"

"Yes."

His lips formed a thin line. "It *is* hard to swallow."

She nodded. "But true, nonetheless."

"So, why is it so important to discuss this now?"

"I'm not sure. You asked me to live with you. You should know that's a pretty significant step for me. Though my mother pretty much operates that way, I've never lived with any of my lovers. It never seemed... necessary." She straightened. "Did you live with April?"

"No."

"See? What you're asking is huge. I just want to make sure you're getting the whole picture here."

His eyes darkened. "I understand. You're afraid I'll get too attached."

Her eyes misted and a whirlwind of confusion rose in her. Why was it so hard with him? She'd never had all this drama with her past loves. "My relationships with men do tend to be temporary."

A sound of choked disbelief burst from him. "Tell that to all your *friends* you've still got hanging around."

"You know what I mean—my romantic relationships. After the healing is complete the nature of the relationship changes. Honestly, since I've been with you I hardly see the others anymore. But you should know that in the past it's always been a mutual breakup."

He sat with his head bowed for an indeterminate time. Did he mean not to respond? Then he raised his head. "And when we reach that mutually agreeable breakup, then you would move on to the next man in need of healing?"

Her throat tightened. "Yes, that's usually the way it works."

His shoulders heaved as he inhaled a deep breath

and straightened. "Okay. I'm still willing to give it a try. So, what's it going to be, Tess? Will you, or will you not live with me?"

THE RAIN DESCENDED THAT night, pouring down in torrents as Tess lay awake, staring at the textured pattern of her ceiling. A feeling of impending doom settled over her and she let it take hold, closing her eyes and shuddering.

Move in with me, Tess. Live with me and share my life.

Could she do it? Could she live with Mason? Part of her thrilled at the idea, but another part, a larger part, recoiled from it. Why did the prospect of living with him bother her so much? Maggie lived with her lovers all the time, always had for as far back as Tess could remember, and she'd never seemed to suffer any ill consequences.

Or had she?

Tess threw off the blankets and flopped to her side. Granted, her mother had seemed fine during the cookout—certainly fine enough to participate in Mason's grilling—yet something about her had seemed off. Tess just couldn't put her finger on exactly what bothered her about Maggie's behavior that day. Every time Tess tried to have a word alone with her, her mother had managed to scoot away with one excuse or another.

She obviously was determined not to discuss any of her personal matters with Tess.

"Fine." Tess bunched up her pillow.

And if her mother hadn't given her enough to worry about, Mason had sprung his proposal that they live together on her. She took a deep breath and rolled onto her stomach. The quiet of the apartment closed in on her.

She hated this quiet, hated not having her guys

around. A lump formed in her throat. Why had they deserted her? It had to have something to do with Mason. The timing couldn't be a coincidence. Was this all part of her gift's evolution? If so, was she ready to let her other men go and to fully embrace Mason?

She couldn't deny it. He had changed her gift—changed her. Would their relationship change further if they lived together? Certainly the arrangement indicated a more serious attitude—a more vested interest.

But she had serious relationships all the time. She fell in and out of love as often as she bought new shoes, which, depending on the sales she came across, could be fairly often. This relationship was no more or less serious than the rest. Why did the detail of where she lived have to factor?

She shifted onto her back and blew out a breath, again staring blankly at the textured ceiling. She was fooling herself to think this relationship was like the others. It was something entirely different. Because Mason was a man like none of the others.

And she loved him in a way that she had never loved any man before.

Fear wrapped itself around her. What if she got so caught up in this love affair that she never fell out of love with him? So far, the course of their relationship hadn't followed the norm of her past encounters. Why would it now?

What if there was no happy parting? What if there was no parting at all? It was all well and good for Nikki to give up the gift. She'd never wanted it to begin with.

But Tess had embraced the gift. Even before she'd known of this strange power she'd inherited, she'd thrived on her many romantic encounters. Her whole world revolved around being with the men in her life, and while they were with her, their lives had revolved around her.

With Mason this wasn't the case. He had a life—a very full one—outside of his relationship with her. Where did she fit in with that? She shuddered at the memory of the pizza outing with the teens when she'd felt their emotions battering her to the point that she was drained and beaten. The teens would be at Thursday's planning meeting and she'd have to face them head-on. How was she to do that?

But the biggest question of all wasn't where and how she'd fit into his life. The biggest question roared at her in the darkness. If she stayed with Mason and lost the gift, then who would she be?

"Damn it." She yanked her pillow from under her head, then threw it at the wall.

Until she knew who she was on her own, without her gift, how could she possibly know who she was supposed to be with someone else?

The darkness closed in as sadness engulfed her. She'd promised Mason an answer by Thursday's meeting. And right now there was only one answer that made any sense, as miserable as it might make her.

She had to tell him she couldn't live with him.

"So, HOW DO YOU FEEL about a cup of java?" Mason asked, nodding at a coffee shop as he and Rafe headed home after a second Hurricanes outing the following evening.

Mason had needed to spend some quality time with

Rafe, since he'd been so distracted the last time, and he hoped to get his mind off Tess and the fact that she hadn't yet gotten back to him on his proposal. The least he could do was to buy the kid some coffee.

Rafe nodded. "Sure."

The place was surprisingly busy for a weeknight, teeming with various customers and an abundance of teenagers. Rafe shifted as they stood in line to order, his head down, his shoulders tense. "Maybe we should just take this to go."

Mason frowned. Why did Rafe seem so uneasy? He glanced around at the crowd. "It *is* pretty packed in here. Wonder what the big draw is?"

"It's the movie theater next door. Kids don't have anywhere else to hang."

"Yeah? That's why we need to build the youth center. It's absolutely necessary." He clapped Rafe on the back. "No problem. We can take our coffee on the road."

Rafe nodded, but his discomfort seemed to increase as more kids filed into the place. Something was definitely bothering him.

Mason placed their order, then turned to Rafe. "Are you okay?"

He ducked his head. "Yeah, just a little tired."

"Okay, we'll get this, and then I'll take you straight home."

Rafe nodded.

They grabbed their drinks, then turned to weave their way through the crowd. A knot of tough-looking teenage boys pushed their way toward them. They wore blue bandannas, either covering their hair, tied to a wrist or just hanging from a pocket and they all bore the same shaved stripe in their brows—the same mark Rafe had worn when Mason had first met him.

Rafe stiffened beside him and Mason tensed.

Gangbangers.

Mason faced the four young men as they blocked their way, but Rafe pushed in front of him.

"Yo, guys, what's up?" He raised his hand in greeting and shook the closest kid's hand in a ritual handshake Mason couldn't begin to follow.

The young man's eyes widened, but he went through the motions of the shake with a slow smile. "Yo, Rafe, where you been? We thought maybe you'd cut out of town or something. You been ditchin' us, man?"

"No, I been around. Got myself a job."

"Yeah, and new friends?" One of the other boys threw a snide glance at Mason. "What's up with that?"

"Hi." Mason smiled at the youth, hoping to defuse the tension. "I'm Mason, one of Rafe's new friends." He extended his hand. "Sorry, I just know the standard shake."

The young man stared at Mason's extended hand for one long minute as people moved past them in the coffee shop. Then he gripped his hand. "Yo, I'm Cisco."

Mason held the kid's gaze. "Rafe has been helping me out. I've kept him busy."

"What's the matter, Rafe? We not good enough for you no more?" Another of the kids moved forward.

"No, it's not like that. My old man's been sick again and I've been looking after him." Rafe smiled, though his shoulders remained tense. "So what's up with you?"

"We're headed to a party." The first young man

glanced at Mason, then back at Rafe. "We're thinking you should cruise with us, bro."

Mason put up his hand before Rafe could reply. "I'm sorry. I've got to get Rafe home. I promised his father we wouldn't be late."

"So, this your new baby-sitter, Rafe?" one of the boys asked, his voice taunting.

"He's not my babysitter." Rafe cast Mason a sideways glance and straightened, his chin lifting. "But he's been helping me stay out of trouble."

Sounds of derision and disbelief erupted from the group. The second young man frowned at Rafe. "That's jack, man. You know you can't diss your boys and start hanging with some do-gooder."

"That's not right, man," another said, his expression angry.

Rafe stood his ground. "I'm making something of my life."

"You don't need him—" Cisco jerked his head toward Mason "—to help you make somethin' of yourself. You got us. Pace is always lookin' to take on new boys. I told you I would hook you up."

Rafe pulled back and shook his head in obvious disgust, his hands fisted. "I'm not working for Pace."

Cisco shook his head. "You made your choice, then. You know the price."

Mason surged toward the young man, but Rafe held him back as Cisco and his friends turned to leave.

"Let's go." Rafe's bravado seemed to disappear as he and Mason headed for the car a moment later.

"Rafe, what was that about?"

"Don't worry about it. I can handle it."

Mason waited until they were on the interstate, before turning to the young man. "Look, son, if you're in some kind of trouble—"

"I told you I can handle it. I know what I'm doing." He blew out a breath. "I got to tell you. I wouldn't have stood up to them before—before I met you."

"That was your old gang?"

Rafe stared silently at the road.

"What will they do?"

More silence. Mason shook his head as they took Rafe's exit. "I have plenty of room at my place if you and your dad want to come stay for a while."

For a second, Rafe's shoulders slumped, but then he shook his head. "We're straight."

"Rafe—"

The young man turned to him, his eyes glistening with unshed tears in the dim light. "Have you ever wanted something so bad you hurt with it?"

Mason nodded as he pulled into Rafe's driveway. He let his gaze drift over the iron grillwork covering the windows and his throat tightened. No one should have to live like this. "Yeah, I think I know what you're saying."

"Then you've got to leave me to this. One way or another it'll all be over soon." He slipped from the car.

"Rafe."

Rafe turned, his eyebrows raised in question.

"You watch your back and you call me if you need me."

A slow smile spread across Rafe's face, and for the first time since Mason had met him, the smile reached the boy's eyes. "You got it, Dr. Davies."

Then he turned and headed into the darkness surrounding the house.

A LOUD RINGING JOLTED Tess from a deep sleep. She opened her eyes and groped for the phone on her nightstand as the thing pealed again. She knocked a picture frame and a half-eaten muffin to the floor before she managed to wrestle the phone to her ear.

"Hello?" Squinting, she made out the digital display on her clock that told her it was five-thirty in the morning. Christ, who was calling so early?

"Tess?" Tension vibrated in Mason's voice, bringing her eyes fully open in the predawn darkness.

"Mason?" She struggled through her tangle of blankets to a sitting position. "What's wrong?"

"I'm so sorry to call you. I just wasn't sure what else to do and…" He took a deep breath. "I really needed to hear your voice."

"It's okay. What's happened?"

"It's Rafe. His father just called me. He's missing. I think he's in some kind of trouble."

"What?"

"We went to a game again last night and he seemed to have a good time, then we stopped for coffee afterward and he ran into former friends of his, gangbangers. I think it has to do with Rafe's leaving the gang. They didn't seem so happy about it."

Fear raced up Tess's spine. "Rafe is in a gang?"

"I know that he used to be, though he has always denied it."

"So, how did he get out?"

"I think he just walked away, but I'm afraid his old buddies weren't ready to let him go. I don't know, I've heard some bad stories about what gangs do to members who want out. I talked to the police a little while ago, and though we can't file a missing person's yet, they said they'd keep an eye out for him."

"Oh, Mason, I'm so sorry." A feeling of helplessness settled over her. "I'll be right there."

"Hold on. That might be the police." He clicked over to his other line.

Tess held her breath and made a plea that was as close to a prayer as she'd ever made that they'd find Rafe safe and sound...and soon.

"That was his father. They found him," Mason said as he came back on the line.

She gripped the phone. "How is he?"

"He's at the hospital. He's unconscious."

"Oh, my God, Mason. What happened?"

"They jumped him and beat him out."

"Beat him out?"

"It means he's out of the gang...if he lives."

14

MASON'S THROAT TIGHTENED as he leaned over Rafe. His eyes were swollen shut and his lip broken open. Casts dressed his right arm and left leg, but the bandage around the boy's head gave Mason the most concern.

He pressed his fingers to the young man's throat and let out his breath. His pulse beat a steady rhythm. Glancing over the young man's chart, he frowned. Rafe had a concussion. He'd woken for a short period, but it could take weeks before they saw the full effects.

At least the boy was going to recover. It could have been much worse.

Anger washed over Mason as he stared at the empty chair beside the bed. Where was Rafe's father? Immediately, he shook his head and chastised himself for blaming the man. He'd probably been too ill to visit his son. But Mason's stomach churned as he thought of Rafe lying in the hospital by himself. No one should be left alone like that.

Especially a child.

A soft scraping sounded behind him. He turned to where Tess stood just inside the door. He motioned to her and she moved on unsteady legs toward him, her face pale. Her soft scent drifted over him as he slipped his arm around her and pulled her to his side. "He'll be okay."

She nodded, her eyes brimming with tears as she gazed at the still young man in the bed. "It's just awful…this violence."

"I know he looks bad, sweetheart, but he's really very lucky. He didn't have any internal injuries, aside from the concussion. His age will actually make his recuperation from that a little longer, but there's no reason not to expect him to have a full recovery."

Again she nodded and tried to wipe the moisture from her eyes, but when she took Rafe's good hand in hers, she crumpled to the side of the bed and tears spilled freely down her cheeks.

Alarmed, Mason placed his hand on her shoulder. "Babe, you don't have to be here."

For long moments she sat with her eyes closed, Rafe's hand in hers, her breathing labored. He attempted to pull her away, but she clamped her free hand over his and shook her head. When at last she calmed, she looked at him, her eyes rimmed in red, sorrow engulfing her. Her voice shook as she spoke. "He's had such a hard life."

"Yes, but it's made him tough. That boy's a real scrapper. He'll bounce back. I'm going to do my best to see things go better for him for as long as I can."

"Where is his father?"

Mason shrugged, tamping down the unbidden animosity that rose in him. "I guess he's too ill to come. I'll call him later. I'd better get you home, then I'll come back and stay with him. I don't want him to be alone when he wakes."

"I'll wait with you."

"No." The word burst from him, harsher than he'd intended. "It isn't necessary."

He shook his head, searching for the right words. How to tell her he'd been wrong to call her—that he didn't need her as a distraction now? That seeing her at once made him ache to have her and reminded him of his offer to join his life with hers. That her hesitance in accepting his proposal was as good as any abandonment?

The ache inside him grew. Pain for Rafe. Pain for all the lonely moments in his own life when he'd needed someone there with him.

"I can drive myself home." Her voice sounded drawn. Thin.

"I'll call you later."

He met her gaze and the depth of her grief reached out to him, twisting his gut, baring his soul, until he turned from her, ready to pound the walls with the rage swelling through him. He didn't need her pity.

She stood for a moment in silence, then spoke again, her words stronger. "We're going to have that fancy ball of yours and get that youth center up and running. Maybe if Rafe had had a place like that to go to, then this would never have happened." She lifted her chin high. "You've got my promise that I will do everything in my power to help make that center a reality."

As she turned to leave, a lump formed in Mason's throat. He reached for her, unable to speak, suddenly wanting more than anything for her to stay. She left without looking back and he sank into the chair by the bed.

God, what would he do when his time with her ended?

TESS STOOD OUTSIDE THE meeting room for the Thursday night planning meeting and closed her eyes. For the hundredth time she pushed aside the ache that plagued her each time she thought of Mason and how he'd turned her away at the hospital. Time. He just needed time.

She inhaled a deep breath and focused on the task at hand, envisioning a ball of light all around her. After leaving the hospital the other day she'd gone to see Aunt Sophie, distraught over Rafe and her inability to bear the intensity of emotion that poured into her anytime she came in contact with the youth.

The empathic rush from him had nearly destroyed her in the hospital. It was almost as if she could feel each blow the boy had suffered. Aunt Sophie had suggested she try the ball of light with the teens, while holding the intention that she would feel only what she chose to feel. And though the entire idea sounded a little out there, Tess was determined to try anything that might help her cope with this new quirk of her gift.

Lifting her chin, she squelched the urge to call Mason and beg him to come. His presence had certainly been a stabilizing force for her, especially in the hospital, but he'd spent every spare moment he had this week with Rafe. Since Rafe wasn't yet up to joining them, they'd have to make do without Mason as well.

She pushed open the door and found herself again in the midst of the DCWC. With each planning meeting their numbers grew. An excited buzz filled the air.

Her stomach tightened. Had the teens come? She scanned the room. They sat in a huddled group in a back corner.

Cassie hurried over to her. "Tess, I was afraid you wouldn't make it tonight. How's Rafe?"

"He's home and recovering. Mason's with him."

"Good. Oh, guess who's come to lend a hand?"

"Who?"

Cassie nodded toward a nearby table. Tess followed her gaze to where April sat in deep conversation with a couple of regular attendees. "Well." Tess turned to Cassie. "That's impressive."

"I told you she's not so bad. I knew she'd come around. Lord knows we can use her. Why don't you find a seat? We're almost ready to get started."

"Okay, but first I'm going to check on the kids." She moved toward the back, but a hand on her arm stopped her.

Pam Alberts, communications chair, smiled at her. "Tess, I've been meaning to call you. I understand you're responsible for that wonderful write-up in the *Miami Herald.* What a coup. I have been trying to get them to do a piece on us for years. The exposure is phenomenal."

"Actually, that was Josh's doing."

Glancing around, she spied him amid a swarm of adoring women. She shook her head. No wonder she hadn't heard from him lately. Between his personal training, Erin and the DCWC, he didn't have any time left for her. He waved and she waved back.

"There he is." She pointed Pam in his direction. "He's the guy with all the connections. Trust me, you won't have any trouble with publicity from now on."

"Well, I know he wouldn't be here if not for you. And Cassie says we found the caterer, the orchestra and the decorator all through you, too. How did we ever manage before you came?"

"I think you ladies did just fine."

"Well, if you have time, could you stop by the communications group when we break out? I have a few ideas I want to bounce off you. Maybe Josh can join as well."

A sense of satisfaction surged through Tess. At last the group was appreciating what she brought to the table. She opened her mouth to respond but hesitated, glancing at the back corner. One girl, who sported piercings in her nose and brow, sat with her arms crossed, a sullen expression on her face. Another had her head bent over a notebook, her pencil flying over the page, while a young man, with his dark hair spiked and bleached at the tips, balanced a dagger on the end of his finger.

Finally, she turned to Pam. "I think I'm going to be busy, but Josh can fill me in later."

Without waiting for a reply, she moved past the rows of chairs to the back. She stopped just short of the teens, again imagining the light surrounding her. She cleared her throat and they all glanced at her. "Hi. Remember me?"

The boy laid the knife across his lap and eyed her with interest. "Tess, right? From the beach cleanup."

"Yes, and I'm sorry I don't remember all of your names."

She relaxed a fraction as they each introduced themselves. Only faint glimmers of the turbulence she'd experienced with them before rippled through her. Aunt Sophie's ball of light seemed to be working.

Swallowing, she faced the young man with the knife. "That thing makes me a little nervous. Would you mind putting it away?"

For a long moment he stared at her, his eyebrows furrowed. Traces of resentment flickered from him. The others turned in his direction and tension hummed through the group. Then he slowly stowed the blade in a sheath strapped to his chest under his shirt.

He spread his hands in an open gesture. "So, we ready to get to it, or what? Don't we have a ball to put on or something?"

As the rest of the group turned to her, expectant looks on their faces, Tess breathed a sigh of relief. She pulled out the list Cassie had given her and handed each of them a copy. "Yes, we do, so let's get to it."

"HI." TESS STARED AT MASON the following Wednesday as he stood in her doorway. Relief and joy flooded her. The ball was days away and she'd hardly heard from him since Rafe had gotten hurt. She barely believed he stood there now and she hadn't dreamed him.

"May I come in?"

"Yes. Of course." She moved back and held her breath. Distress still weighed heavy on him. His clothes hung from his body, wrinkled and disheveled.

She opened her arms and he walked into them, scooping her close and burying his face in the crook of her neck. Closing her eyes, she savored the intimacy he offered, cradling him and thankful he had come to her at last.

After a few moments he pulled back, his eyes bloodshot, weariness etched into his face. "God, I missed you."

"Me, too." Her eyes misted and her throat tightened. *Live with me.*

She inhaled a deep breath. "Mason—"

"Shh." He pulled her close again and kissed her, his tongue imploring.

She melted into him—melted into his kiss, giving him all she had to give—her heart bursting with love for him and the hope that maybe, just maybe, one day she could fill the void in his.

Without breaking the kiss, he lifted her and carried her to her room. He laid her on the bed and she took him again into her arms. His stubbled cheek rubbed her face and his voice sounded gruff and hollow in her ear.

"Love me, Tess."

She kissed him then, holding him close, opening her heart to him, offering her soul. She touched him and stroked him, her need for him overwhelming in its intensity. Moments later he seated himself deep inside her and she cried out, tears spilling down her cheeks, his desolation and his joy more than she could bear.

He thrust into her, his eyes closed, his mouth open in a wordless cry. The desire in her rose as his movements took on a primal rhythm and she lost herself in an endless sea of sensation, the turbulence of his emotions washing over her. At last unrestrained, he gave her all he had—his loneliness, his grief and a love powerful enough to steal her breath. He thrust again and cried out in a release so strong it left her weeping as he collapsed, spent, beside her.

She lay awake late into the night, memorizing the serene lines of his face. At long last she slept, her arm draped over him, her heart filled with peace. When she woke in the early hours just past dawn, he was gone.

MUSIC SWELLED ACROSS THE ballroom. Mason glanced through the crowd of black ties and sequined gowns, straining for a glimpse of Tess. Apprehension filled him. She'd insisted on arriving before him, citing the excuse that she and the teens needed to help her sister with final touches on the decorations.

He closed his eyes as snatches of his last night with her flashed before him. He'd been exhausted and worn when he'd gone to her. The memory blurred in his mind, a collage of heat and despair…and tranquility. A tremor of remorse ran through him. He'd taken her in pain and anger and she'd given him peace.

Opening his eyes, he looked again for her. Now that Rafe was recovering, Mason needed to set things right with Tess. He didn't want to push her into a decision to live with him, but now that the question was out there, it seemed to hang between them.

Hopefully tonight she'd put him out of his misery, one way or another.

A flash of white in the black-and-jewel-toned crowd caught his eye and he moved toward her, anxious to see if she might have an answer.

"Wonderful party, Mason, dear." An older woman, her silver hair swept up in a complicated twist, laid her well-manicured hand on his arm.

He scoured his memory for her name. "Thank you, Mrs. Brandywine. I'm so glad you and Dr. Brandywine were able to make it."

"Once he heard Dawn Bailey was dragging Phillip here, George wouldn't have missed it for anything."

"Their attendance is a boon for us. They seem to have drawn quite a number of admirers."

"Your success is practically guaranteed. I hear Dawn has taken quite an interest in your Project Mentor."

"Yes, I understand she stopped by one of the teen workshops last week."

"The word I have is that she was quite impressed." She glanced past his shoulder. "Oh, there she is. If you'll excuse me, Mason, I'd like a word with her."

"No problem, I'd like a word with her myself to thank her for her interest."

Mrs. Brandywine waved goodbye, then disappeared into the crowd. Mason peered through the shifting revelers to where a stately woman smiled at Mrs. Brandywine.

He would have to meet with Dawn Bailey later. For now, he needed to find Tess. Glancing around, he caught another glimpse of her and moved in that direction, smiling and nodding as he passed various attendees. At last, he came to the edge of the dance floor, where couples moved to a waltz.

Mason steeled himself against the sight of Tess laughing and gazing into the eyes of another man while he swept her across the polished floor. Mason's stomach tightened. How could he have let himself forget how she collected men like so many knickknacks?

My relationships with men do tend to all be temporary.

Gritting his teeth, he pushed past swirling couples to tap the man on his shoulder.

It was Max, from the cookout, and he turned, eyebrows raised. "Hey, Mason, what's up?"

Mason leveled his gaze on him. "I'm cutting in."

"Oh, right." He turned to Tess and kissed her cheek. "I'll talk to you later, sweetie."

Anger boiled up inside Mason as he took Tess in his arms. Maybe Max was the reminder he needed that Tess might not be the woman for him. Yet as she rested her hand in his, that soothing feeling that always accompanied her drifted over him, calming him.

You don't want to believe it, but you can't dispute the fact that something unusual, something maybe even magical, happens when we're together.

Was it true? Was she really a healer—a sexual healer?

Another couple swept by and the man winked at her. Resentment rose in Mason as he glared at the man. Damn it, he just couldn't wait anymore. "Tess, I have to know if you've made a decision."

She drew back, her eyes wide. "You mean about your proposal that we live together?"

"Yes."

"I was going to talk to you about it before, but then all that happened with Rafe and…"

"And?"

"I don't know that this is the proper time and place."

He would have laughed had he had any humor left in him. "*Now* you get a social conscience?"

"We've worked so hard for this night."

"And you don't want to ruin it by telling me it isn't going to work between us?"

She stopped in the middle of the dance floor. "No, that isn't what I was going to say."

"Then what were you going to say? Will you or will you not live with me?"

"It isn't that easy. I don't think you've thought this through."

"That's a no."

Her eyes glistened under the huge globe lights. "It doesn't mean I don't want to still be with you."

Disappointment clawed its way through him. His stomach constricted. He'd known from the moment he'd asked her that she'd say no. Who was he kidding? He'd taken his walk on the wild side, but the wild side hadn't welcomed him.

He stepped away from her. "Excuse me, I need to get some air."

"Mason, wait, I want to explain."

"No, don't...it's okay. It doesn't matter."

Before she could respond, he made his way toward the heavy double doors leading out of the ballroom. He avoided eye contact with everyone on his way, focusing only on the exit.

"Mr. Bailey, wait. Please, don't go." April crossed in front of him, her arms outstretched toward a bull of a man.

Mason pulled up short. "April?"

"Mason." She turned back to the man as he stopped in front of them, her eyes wide and a note of panic in her voice. "Mr. Bailey, surely you realize the Dade County Women's Club and Project Mentor don't condone such activities."

"What activities?" Mason asked. What the hell was going on?

"That woman—that gypsy..." Outrage shone in Phillip Bailey's eyes as he shook a heavy finger toward the back of the ballroom. He turned, scowling, toward Mason. "Mason Davies?"

"Yes, sir, I'm Mason Davies." He extended his hand. "What seems to be the problem?"

The man narrowed his eyes, the muscles in his neck bulging. "You can kiss that youth center goodbye."

Mason straightened and cast April a sideways glance. She spread her hands in a helpless gesture. "Whatever the issue, I'm sure we can work this out, Mr. Bailey. Why don't you let me get you a drink?"

"I don't need a drink. I need to get the hell out of here. What a bunch of— Good night, Dr. Davies. This meal ticket is out of here." Without another word, Bailey stormed out the door.

Mason stared after him in dismay, then his gaze shifted over the small crowd that had gathered around them. He turned to April. "What was that about?"

Tess caught up to him. "Mason, please, let's go someplace where we can talk."

"Hold on." He said to April, "What activities do we not condone? What gypsy woman was he talking about?"

April cast Tess a nervous glance. "I'm so sorry, but it's her people. I'm afraid they've ruined it all for us."

Tess looked from April to Mason. "What is she talking about?"

April raised her hands in distress. "Your aunt—I believe that's who she is—is the one he called a gypsy woman. She has run off our most promising benefactor."

"Aunt Sophie?" Tess's gaze narrowed. "You can't be serious. Aunt Sophie wouldn't do that."

"She certainly did. She's selling her services at one of the banquet tables, giving some kind of card readings to all the guests."

Tess shook her head. "That's harmless and I'm sure she wouldn't charge a fee. She never does."

"I don't think Phillip Bailey thought it was harmless. She told him something about abusing his power and using manipulation for his own gains. I don't know exactly what she said, but couldn't she have made up something good? He was livid when he stomped out of here." April wrung her hands. "Without his donation we can't possibly make our goal now."

Mason stared at the board at the front of the ballroom that tallied the donations in a digital display. They were well below the halfway mark. April was right. They *had* been counting on a donation from the Baileys to put them over the top.

A sick feeling twisted through him as a vision of Rafe in his hospital bed flickered through his mind.

He'd failed the kids.

"That's ridiculous." Tess stepped forward, steeled for battle. "Whatever Aunt Sophie told him, it was something he needed to hear. She couldn't just make it up. She has too much integrity for that. If Bailey chooses to listen to her, her readings always prove helpful. She has never hurt a soul through them."

"You didn't see him." April faced her, fists clenched. "He was to be this project's main benefactor. Am I not right, Mason? Without his support we're dead in the water."

"That can't be true." Tess turned to Mason, her eyes liquid blue. "Mason?"

Mason nodded, feeling numb and sick with the taste of defeat.

"No." Tess touched his arm and he shifted away from her. "The night isn't over, there's still a chance. I'll get up and make a speech, implore everyone to dig deep and give for the children."

Light reflected off the diamond studs in April's ears as she shook her head. "Cassie's been up there all night. She does this for all the DCWC fund-raisers. If she can't charm the money out of them, it isn't going to happen."

"But there's still time."

April gripped Mason's arm as she glanced uneasily

at the murmuring crowd. "We might still scrounge enough to put together another fund-raiser, but…" Again her gaze skittered to Tess. "I'm really sorry, Tess, but we've got to take care of this problem first."

Frowning, Mason turned to April. "What do you mean? What problem?"

"Well, if we're going to salvage anything of this night, it seems to me we have just one hope. I hate to say it, but…but…" She took a deep breath. "Well, I think it would be best if Tess took her aunt and the rest of her family out of here. They should probably all leave."

"What?" Tess stared at her, her eyes round in disbelief.

Ask Tess and her family to leave? Mason shook his head. How could he do such a thing?

"If they don't, then we'll ruin our chances of salvaging anything out of this fiasco. Look at this crowd. They don't look so happy. A lot of people witnessed the event and this place is filled with Bailey's supporters. I'm sure they're waiting to see how we respond." She said to Tess, "You have to understand that we need to cut our losses."

"Mason." Tess touched his arm again. "You know that isn't true. There are still plenty of people left. The night is young. Let me—"

"She's right." Mason closed his eyes against the memory of Rafe facing off with the gangbangers who put him in the hospital.

"You want us to leave?" Tess's voice shook.

He swallowed past a lump in his throat. The room blurred. This was for the best. He had to think of the youth center. Besides, Tess had rejected him, as he'd known all along she would.

Mason had to cut his losses in more than one way.

It should end things between them nicely. Then he could get on with his life. He met her gaze. "Yes, I want you all to leave."

She stood still for one unbelieving moment, then she fled into the dwindling crowd.

TESS SWEPT THE SKIRT of her dress aside and plopped down on Sophie's couch. Anger raged through her. She drew it around her like a cloak, protecting her from the despair lingering just beneath it. "I still can't believe it."

Erin shook her head as she settled beside her. "Men. They just aren't worth a damn. I'm convinced we don't need them."

Sophie set her requisite tea tray on the table and settled beside Maggie, who'd remained home for the evening with the vague excuse that she had plans. "Don't be silly. I spent half my life believing men needed us, but I am convinced we need them every bit as much."

Erin rolled her eyes. Maggie snorted but refrained from comment. She seemed to grow less outspoken every day. Forgetting her own frustrations for the moment, Tess leaned forward but was still unable to get anything from either her mother or Aunt Sophie.

"I don't know." Tess flopped against the cushion. Sadness seeped through her anger. She closed her eyes a moment until the burning in her throat lessened. "I wouldn't say that I needed Mason, exactly, but there was definitely something different about him."

"Like what, dear? I couldn't quite put my finger on it before." Maggie sipped tea from a special mug Sophie had brought her.

"I don't know. It was like I felt…different when I was with him."

"What do you mean, 'different'?" Erin asked.

Tess glanced around at the questioning faces. "It's hard to explain, but I guess he made me feel…better, maybe? Except for tonight," she added with a bitter note. Tonight he had effectively crumbled her foundation beneath her. "I know it sounds corny, but sometimes I felt uplifted, like…"

"Like you could conquer the world?" Sophie asked, her eyebrows arched.

"Yes, I guess so. What does it mean?"

Sophie frowned. "I'm not sure. Like I keep saying, you girls are a whole new breed, so to speak, but my guess is that in certain instances, it's possible that the healer receives some sort of reciprocal healing."

"Reciprocal healing?" Maggie leaned forward. "That would seem to go hand in hand with the empathic nature. Don't you think?"

"That's probably right." Sophie nodded. "If the healer can feel the emotions of the healee, then why not the healing energy?"

Tess frowned. "But if that's the case, then why wouldn't it work like that every time?"

Sophie shrugged. "Not sure."

"Not that I'm buying into any of this, but maybe it's a matter of the energy flow having the proper conduit." Erin glanced at each of them in turn.

Maggie twisted a lock of her hair around her finger. "Meaning it would only work with the right man?"

Erin nodded. "It's just a theory."

"Well, it's a moot point now." Tess stared into her

empty cup. "I'm guessing after tonight, things are effectively over with Mason. I can't believe he asked me—all of us—to leave like that."

Sophie patted her knee. "You need not worry, dear. His actions tonight show that he is in dire need of your healing."

"Do you know that he asked me to live with him and I had actually given it serious consideration?"

Maggie shrugged. "I always found that living with them helped the healing."

"Well, it isn't happening now. No way." Tess folded her arms. No need to tell them all she had already turned him down. Didn't need to stir that pot.

What an idiot she'd been. Moisture gathered in her eyes and her throat tightened. "I've never been so humiliated. How could he let anyone talk about you like that, Aunt Sophie? April accused you of ruining the fund-raiser."

"Why would she say that?" Maggie asked.

"Some bigwig potential benefactor didn't like a reading I gave him."

"You were giving readings at the ball?" Maggie turned wide-eyed to Sophie.

"I told them anything you said was something that man needed to hear," Tess said.

"So he left without making a donation?" Erin asked.

Tess nodded. "According to April the man was livid. Apparently they were counting on his contribution."

"He made a contribution," Sophie said.

"Then it wasn't enough. The board wasn't even to the halfway point when we left." Disappointment flooded Tess. Not only had the night ended her relationship with Mason, it may have been the end of Project Mentor. "I guess there won't be a youth center, after all."

A mysterious smile lit Sophie's face. "Oh, I wouldn't be so sure about that."

"Why not?" Tess asked.

"You see, I told everyone that I would give the proceeds from the readings to Project Mentor."

Tess straightened. "So how much did you charge?"

"The usual love offering. I left it up to each individual to decide, based on how they liked the reading."

"How much did you donate?"

"Let's see…" Sophie quirked her lips as she made a mental calculation. "I would say that the amount I dropped in the box on our way out should have put you just over the top of your goal."

Tess stared, stunned. "Oh, my God, Aunt Sophie. You have got to be kidding."

"Not at all. I had some serious customers tonight and they went away quite pleased. Set a good number of them straight." She shrugged. "With the exception of that Bailey character, of course."

"But you said that he made a contribution," Erin reminded her.

"Oh, he did. After he ran off in a huff that gracious wife of his made an extremely generous love offering and she insisted it was with his money."

"Good for her." Erin nodded her satisfaction.

In spite of the gloom that had settled over her, excitement glimmered through Tess. "So, what you're saying is that we've got our youth center."

"That's right, but you do know what else this means?"

Tess frowned. "What?"

"It means that man is going to need you more than ever now."

15

THE CROWD IN THE BALLROOM erupted in applause. Mason stared, astounded at the flashing numbers on the board at the front of the room. If the numbers were correct, they'd surpassed their goal.

It couldn't be.

He glanced around for Cassie Aikens. Cassie would surely know if there had been a mistake. He straightened as she stepped up to the microphone on the podium at the front. The roar of the crowd settled as she tapped the microphone to get their attention.

"Good evening, everyone." She gestured to the board behind her. "It looks like we made it."

The crowd went wild in its enthusiastic response. Cassie smiled and nodded as the commotion settled down. "We have so many people to thank." She gestured to the long list of names displayed beside the tally.

Mason's stomach constricted. The last name listed was Sophie Patterson. Tess's aunt had made a donation?

"For all of you who had readings by Sophie Patterson, you should know that Sophie's was the final donation that put us over the top. She donated all the proceeds from her readings and evidently she had some very pleased customers."

The crowd again erupted in applause. Mason shook his head, incredulous. He'd asked Tess and her family to leave because he'd thought they had spoiled their best shot at earning the money for the center.

Instead, they actually had cinched it for them.

"I'll be damned." April moved beside Mason. "That can't be right."

Mason gave her a long look. What a fool he'd been. How had he fallen in again with the same old closed-minded thinking? Had April always been so ready to blame others? "Sounds about right to me, April. It appears that we've got our youth center and we didn't need Phillip Bailey to get it."

April straightened. "Well, it's a good thing—for the kids. But you were still right to ask Tess and her group to leave."

"How can you say that? Tess's aunt was one of the highest contributors. I think I've just made the biggest mistake of my life."

"That's nonsense, Mason. I'm sure they'll understand that it was a simple misunderstanding." She slipped her arm through his. "Let's get a drink to celebrate. You'll see. It's all okay."

"No, it isn't." He extricated himself from her grip as he pinned his gaze on her, the truth hitting him in an excruciating flash. "I've just screwed myself royally. You know Tess, the woman I just shoved right out of my life?"

"She's not your type. No one knows you better than me. You're better off without her."

"There's no doubt *she's* better off without me, but you're wrong about me being better off without her. You see, I love her."

April shook her head, her eyes round in disbelief. "You're just confused."

"No, I'm not."

Slowly, she nodded as her eyes glistened. "Then you should go after her."

Mason fisted his hands and stared a long moment at the door. What would going after her gain him? At best a short reprieve in his time with her. In the end she would still leave him. It was in her nature—her healing nature.

He shook his head and turned from the door, all the anger and hurt that had filled him when she'd walked out of that hospital room without a backward glance reclaiming him. It was better this way.

Maybe some wounds never healed.

REJECTION. HOW THE HELL did people deal with it? Tess swigged a long swallow of chocolate milk the following Tuesday night and grabbed a bag of peanut butter cookies from the pantry. A wave of despair washed over her as she shuffled barefoot into her bedroom, letting tears run freely down her cheeks.

She ripped opened the bag of cookies and crawled into her bed, torturing herself with memories of Mason. Snippets of her time with him flashed through her mind like some grotesque kaleidoscope.

Move in with me, Tess. Live with me and share my life.

He'd been so full of hope and caring.

And you don't want to ruin it by telling me it isn't going to work between us?

Why had she been so quick to turn him down?

Yes, I want you all to leave.

Bastard.

The agony hit her again, and she curled into a ball under her blanket. Oh, God, how did anyone survive this?

The ringing of her doorbell brought her out of her unhappy reverie. She bit into a cookie and frowned at the clock. Nine o'clock. Wasn't everyone else in the world out doing something wild and fun? Even Erin had gone to dinner with Josh to celebrate finishing whatever job they'd been working on.

The bell pealed again. Curiosity got the better of her. With a quick slurp from her chocolate milk, she closed up the cookie bag, then blew her nose. Sighing, she padded down the hall to the door as an insistent tapping sounded.

"Tess, open up. I know you're in there." Cassie's muffled voice penetrated the solid wood.

"Cassie?" What the hell? Tess yanked open the door.

Cassie stood on the other side, a bulging grocery bag in one hand, an overflowing video store bag in the other. Erin stood beside her, digging through her purse, evidently for her key.

Tess blinked. "Erin? I thought you were out with Josh."

Her sister shrugged. "We got done early. I thought I'd see what you were up to. Have you got the phone off the hook? I've been trying to call. And check your cell phone. I think your battery's dead again." Her eyebrows arched as she took in Tess's rumpled sweats. "I didn't know you were expecting company."

"I wasn't."

"I tried to call, too. I brought face masks." Cassie indicated a bag slung over her shoulder.

"Face masks?" Tess gestured them to come in, and they filed into the entryway.

"And my pedicure-manicure set." Cassie pawed through the bag. "Oh, and curlers."

"Curlers?" Tess frowned. "Cassie, what is all this?"

Cassie's eyes widened. "Well, girls' night, of course."

"Girls' night?" Tess parroted, feeling like an idiot for repeating everything Cassie said, but she couldn't quite wrap her mind around this sudden turn of events.

"Munchies, movies, mud masks…" Erin's voice was filled with anticipation.

"Girls' night," Cassie offered, and bit her lip. "If you're up to it."

"Tess," Erin said. "You've been moping around since…well, since—"

"Since that old fart, Mason, dumped you." Empathy filled Cassie's voice.

Tess stared at them. "I've been sort of hanging out…."

"Hon, it's perfectly understandable," Cassie said. "One time I was dating this guy I was completely in love with. I was over the moon. Anyway, he dumped me. Just like that."

Erin puckered her lips and shook her head. Tess frowned. "That's…bad."

"Exactly. I crawled into my bed with a stash of cupcakes and potato chips and I didn't come out for a week."

Erin bobbed her head in agreement. "That's exactly what she's been doing. It's horrible. She's an absolute mess."

Cassie shivered visibly. "April pulled me out of it with a girls' night. It was exactly what I needed."

"Oh." Tess's throat tightened and the room turned into a watery blur. Cassie had come to have a girls' night. With her. "I—I don't know what to say."

"Sweetie, you don't have to say anything. If we can't be there for our girlfriends, then what good are we?"

"G-girlfriends?" Fresh tears tracked down Tess's cheeks.

Erin threw her arm around Tess's shoulder. "Hey, I'm up for a girls' night. Shall I call Nikki?"

"Um, sure." Tess scrubbed her hands over her cheeks as happiness bubbled up inside her.

She had a friend—a girlfriend. And Erin and maybe Nikki were joining in on their girls' night.

She peered in Cassie's bag. "I'm on sugar overload. Got any cheese puffs in there?"

TESS STRETCHED AND SLOWLY rose from the bed the following day. She cocked her head. Birdsong sounded outside her window. The air conditioner hissed through the vents, but other than that, silence blanketed her apartment.

She stood for a moment, misery wrapping around her. She missed her guys. Where was everyone? Where was the clink of dishes in the kitchen as Ramon whipped up a breakfast treat? Where was the steady whir of whatever power tool Max might be wielding for the day? And where was Erin, muttering her complaints about all the noise and constant lack of privacy?

They'd stayed up late watching the movies Cassie had brought. It had been in the wee hours when Cassie had turned down her invitation to spend the night and Erin had headed for bed. Maybe she was there still, sleeping in for a change.

Tess sank back onto the bed. She was alone. She could feel the emptiness of the apartment. Her guys were giving her a break, or maybe they were gone for good since Mason had walked into her life and everything had started changing. Erin was either asleep—she glanced at the clock and shook her head—or gone to work on one of her design projects.

Evan had the nursery covered. Tess had nothing pressing to do. She stared up at the ceiling, her day stretching before her, with no one to guide its unfolding but her.

With a slow smile, she rose, then headed for the bathroom. She'd shower, dress, then see where the day took her. A thought struck her. She'd go find Mason's teens. She had all their contact numbers. Maybe in the hours to come she'd find some little part of herself she'd been missing.

"SO, HERE WE ARE." Tess settled on the couch beside the huge bowl of popcorn that sat on the cushion beside Erin later that night. "What are we watching?"

Erin shrugged and clicked a few buttons on the remote. "Not much. How do you feel about reality shows?"

"No good movies on?"

"Let's see." Erin scanned a few more channels. "You know, he's going to call. I'm surprised he hasn't come by. Maybe he did, but you were too busy wallowing in despair to hear him knocking."

"Who?"

"Mason. In fact, I'll bet he's already tried to reach you. You left the computer on with the call-waiting active. You know that screws up the phone. And have you charged your cell phone yet?"

Tess shrugged and scooped up a handful of popcorn. "Doesn't matter to me either way."

"Sure it does. You want him to call. Admit it."

"I'm not admitting any such thing. What's that?"

Erin scanned back a couple of channels. "This? I know, it's that movie with what's his name."

"*Life as a House.* Leave it."

"He must have felt like a complete idiot."

"Who? Kevin Kline?"

"No. Mason. I would have loved to see his face when he found out how much Aunt Sophie donated."

"Yeah, well that was nearly a week ago. If he tried to reach me, he didn't make much of an effort. I haven't left the house."

"Maybe not, but he owes you an apology."

"He did what he thought was best."

"How can you defend him? I mean, I wasn't thrilled when Aunt Sophie broke out the tarot deck, but I don't think it called for him kicking us out."

"He didn't kick us out."

"You said he asked us to leave. Same difference. I can't believe you're defending that man. It's worse than I thought."

"I'm not defending him. I'm doing my best to see his side here. You don't understand. Mason is...complicated."

"Complicated, scmomplicated. The man doesn't deserve you. You are so much better off without him."

Tess popped a kernel of popcorn into her mouth, then another, then another, until she had a mouthful. She chewed with deliberate slowness, then swallowed. *Was* she better off without him?

"I spent the entire day by myself today," she said at

last, scooping up another handful of popcorn. "Well, almost the entire day."

"Really?" Erin turned to look at her, her head cocked. "What did you do?"

"I went for a long walk, checked out the library—"

"The library? Do you even have a card?"

"I do now. They had this entire section on nonprofits. I checked out a couple of books on grant writing." She shrugged. "Even with the start-up money, the youth center is going to need some ongoing funding. I figure I'll check with whoever has started the grant writing and see if they need any help." She gazed at the popcorn in her hand. "I can't let my breakup with Mason stand in the way of any contribution I can make for the kids."

"That's really awesome, Tess."

"That's not all. I went to see Rafe and he is doing so much better. Then I rounded up the other teens and we had an impromptu workshop."

"Doing what?"

"We walked through the park and I taught them about plants. You know, the different herbs you can find pretty much anywhere and what they were used for. They were really into it. We're going to do a class where we make salves and lotions from some of the specimens we collected."

"Wow." Erin grinned at her. "So, it's not just about your men anymore."

"Men? What men?"

"What did Aunt Sophie mean when she said we needed men as much as they needed us? I'm a little surprised she would see it that way. She's always been so independent. Have you ever seen her needing a man?"

"I don't know. I don't always get her, but she usually ends up right in the long run." Tess bit her lip. "Has Nikki said anything to you about Mom?"

Erin heaved a big sigh. "I noticed she seemed a little worn out lately and mentioned it to Thomas. He told me about her fight with Aunt Sophie. I'm assuming it has something to do with that."

"Yeah, I think— Well, Nikki and I both think there's something wrong with Mom. Aunt Sophie is helping her, but they're keeping it to themselves. I don't know, I guess they don't want to worry us." She glanced at her sister. "Nikki's empathic abilities have changed and I never could read the two of them. How about you? Can you read them?"

Erin rolled her eyes the way she did whenever discussion on the gift arose. "You know how I feel about all of that. You may all believe you've been gifted with whatever healing, sensory thingy you have, but I promise you, none of that has come my way."

"Maybe you just haven't, I don't know…woken it up yet, or something."

"Or something," Erin muttered, frowning. "Why didn't you say something to me sooner about Maggie?"

"Well, I didn't know what to tell you, because I don't know what's going on—"

"But you're pretty sure something's going on and you didn't say anything. Don't you think I have the right to know if you and Nikki are worried about our mother?"

Tess heaved a sigh. "I'm sorry, Erin. You're right. It's just that you've been so busy and I didn't want to worry you. And then the thing with Rafe, then Mason dumping me. Besides, we may be getting all tied up about nothing."

"If it was nothing, you and Nikki wouldn't be fretting over it. You're the ones with the extrasensory thing. I just wish for once you two would treat me like the adult I am and discuss these things with me."

"That's what I'm doing."

Erin narrowed her eyes.

"You're right. I'm sorry. I promise, from now on we'll include you right from the start."

"Good. Okay, why don't we just ask Maggie point blank what's going on?"

"We did."

"And?"

"And she said she wasn't going to tell us. It was between her and Aunt Sophie only."

"Well, ask again."

"Have you tried to pin her down lately? She's as slippery as an eel. First we'd have to catch her. Frankly, I don't know if I'm up to that."

"So, let's figure out a way to get her to talk to us. The least we can do is try."

"How are we going to do that?"

"Where's the phone? Let's get Nikki and Thomas over here and we'll see what we can come up with."

"Oh, I have an idea already."

"Yeah? What is it?"

"What draws Maggie like nothing else? What is it that she absolutely can't resist?"

"I don't know…men?"

"Not just any kind of men. We need a man in need of healing. We need Thomas."

"What's wrong with Thomas?"

A slow smile curved her lips. "Nothing…yet."

"I JUST DON'T FEEL RIGHT about this. She'll be able to tell that I'm faking it." Thomas folded his arms and frowned at Tess, Nikki and Erin.

"Think of it as an intervention of sorts. We can't help Mom if we don't know what's troubling her." Tess stirred the teacup Nikki handed her. "Besides, you won't exactly be faking it."

Thomas's eyes narrowed. "What does that mean? What have you got there?"

"Just a little something I brewed up for you." She sniffed the steam coming off the cup. "It's really not so bad and its effects are temporary."

"What effects?"

Nikki sat down beside him. "Nothing to get too concerned about. It's just a special tea Tess accidentally blended when she first started studying herbs with Aunt Sophie."

"It was supposed to help alleviate headaches, but I mistook one herb for another—"

"And she found the perfect brew for us to use whenever we wanted to skip school."

"You mean that mysterious ailment Maggie would fret over when you'd break out in a fever with that awful rash?" He stared at them aghast.

"You knew?" Erin asked. "I didn't even know. They didn't tell me about it until recently."

"No, but it makes sense. Maggie never understood how you could be so sick one minute, then it would clear up so quickly. You won't be able to fool her with that. She'll figure it out, just like I did."

"We only need to get her here." Tess gave Thomas the look that had worked on more men than she could remember.

"No, no, don't do that." He put up his hand as if to ward her off.

"Please, Thomas." Erin gave him her version of the look, her green eyes wide.

"Yes, Thomas, say you'll do it. We're really counting on you," Nikki added.

Thomas groaned and threw up his hands in defeat. "There isn't a man alive who could stand up to the three of you. You girls aren't playing fair."

"But you care about Mom as much as we do." Tess placed the cup in his hand.

"The rash doesn't even itch," Nikki encouraged as he raised the cup and took an exploratory sniff.

"What's in it?" he asked.

"Don't worry," Tess said. "I promise that it's completely safe."

She held her breath as he downed the drink in one long draught, then turned excitedly to her youngest sister. "Erin, you call her. She won't suspect anything if it's you."

"Wait, what if she picks up that I'm not really upset?" She shoved the phone at Tess. "You're the one who learned about that shielding thing."

"What shielding thing?" Nikki asked, but Tess waved her question aside as she punched in her mother's cell phone number and visualized a screen of light cloaking her.

Maggie's phone rang and Tess held her breath. Would her shield work with her mother?

Maggie's cell phone rang a second time and Thomas clutched his head and groaned. "What have you girls done to me?"

"Oh, look." Erin clapped a hand over her mouth and nodded toward Thomas. A bright rash had spread across his neck and was creeping up his face.

"Tess, how long did you steep those leaves?" Nikki's voice carried a note of concern.

"Hello?" Maggie sounded sluggish, as though she'd been sleeping.

"Mom? Did I wake you?"

"Tess? No, I was just resting. Doing a little meditation. What's up?"

"Nikki, Erin and I stopped in to see Thomas and he's not doing so well." She flinched as a red welt bubbled up on Thomas's nose.

"Oh, my, what's wrong with him?" Concern laced Maggie's voice.

"He's sick, Mom. He's burning up and he has this rash. Yuck, he's not looking so good. I think you should come right away."

A short silence hummed across the connection and Tess closed her eyes and focused on her shield of light, then Maggie let out a tired breath. "Okay, sweetie, tell Thomas I'll be right there."

"Great. I'll tell him." Tess disconnected and grinned triumphantly at the others. "It worked. She's on her way. She should be here any minute."

"Thank God," Thomas groaned as Erin placed a cool cloth on his head.

"Jeez, Tess, are you sure you know what you're doing?" Erin asked. "He looks terrible. No offense, Thomas."

Thomas just groaned in response and Tess glanced

at Nikki. Maybe she *had* made the tea a little strong. "He's a big guy, I just thought…"

"He'll be fine," Nikki assured her, then straightened when the front door slammed.

They had time to exchange one nervous glance before Maggie strode into the room, looking as hale and hearty as she had ever looked.

"Thomas?" She went straight to him and dropped to her knees in front of him, placing her hand on his forehead. "Goodness, you *are* burning up."

She turned to Tess. "What have you given him?"

Tess stared, stunned. Busted, right off the bat. "It was just—"

"Some ibuprofen." Nikki gave her a meaningful look. "We thought it might help with the fever, and an antihistamine for the rash, right, Tess?"

"Oh, yeah, right." Tess folded her arms and sat back as Maggie turned to fuss over Thomas.

"Oh, dear, when did this start?" She soothed her hand along his cheek, her voice filled with concern.

Thomas gazed at Maggie, an adoring look in his eyes, in spite of the misery he was surely feeling. "It came on pretty sudden, but I'll be okay."

"Of course you will. I'm going to stay right here and take care of you for as long as you need me."

"Ah, Maggie, love, I'd be lost without you." He pressed his hand over hers.

Tess stared at the two in wonder. How had she never seen it before? She glanced at Nikki to see if her sister might be picking up on the same thing.

Maggie and Thomas?

Nikki's eyebrows arched, and she nodded as her gaze drifted to the two.

"I'll go get him some water." Erin rose.

"Wait a minute, young lady." Maggie cocked her head and assessed her youngest daughter for a long moment, while Erin visibly squirmed.

With a gasp, Maggie swung around toward Nikki and Tess, her eyes narrowed. "I can't believe this." She rose and stepped away from Thomas. "This is a setup."

Thomas flopped back on the cushion. "I told you it wouldn't work."

"And you're in on it, Thomas?" Maggie glared at him. "Someone had better tell me what this is all about and they'd better start talking now."

Tess faced her mother. "It was my idea. I'm sorry. They just all went along with it."

"Tess? What were you thinking?" Maggie gestured to Thomas. "You did...*this* to Thomas? On purpose?"

"We just want to talk to you. We want to know what's wrong and why you and Sophie are all clammed up about it. We all love you and we have a right to know what's happening."

Maggie stood for a moment, her chin high, her hands fisted on her hips as though she were ready to do battle, then she crumpled onto the sofa beside Thomas. "It's no use. You'll all figure it out sooner or later."

Thomas sat up and soothed his hand over hers. The rash had already begun to fade. "What is it, Mags? You can tell us. We're all here for you."

She nodded and a tear slipped down her cheek. "I didn't want to worry any of you."

Tess went to her mother, kneeling in front of her.

"Whatever it is, we want to help. You don't have to go through it on your own."

Maggie's shoulders heaved. "That's what Sophie said."

"Well, Sophie is usually right," Nikki chided from Thomas's other side.

"Yeah, we'll do whatever you need us to." Erin sank into the chair beside the sofa.

"What is it, sweetheart?" Thomas stroked her back.

"What? You're all having a party and you didn't invite me?" Sophie stood in the room's archway. She shrugged. "I saw all the cars."

"Tell them, Sophie," Maggie said.

Sophie nodded and pulled an ottoman close to the group and plopped herself down. "I had a feeling you'd all do something like this. I told her you should know, but she was worried about everyone pitying her or trying to do everything for her."

She paused while she took a deep breath and gazed at her sister, her eyes misting. Maggie reached out and squeezed her hand. "It'll be okay. Tell them."

Sophie straightened. "There's some sort of irreversible separation in her optic nerves. She's going blind."

"Blind?" Tess looked at her mother, alarm and surprise and disbelief all swirling through her.

"Can't they do something?" Erin asked.

Maggie shook her head. "You think all that gallivanting around the world was for the fun of it? No, I've been to the best of the best. There isn't anything anyone can do."

"But surely they can delay it, slow it down. There must be some procedure." Nikki's voice cracked and she pressed her lips together.

"Well, they don't have a specific time frame, but my peripheral vision is already going."

Tess stared at her, aghast. "But your painting."

Maggie waved aside her concern. "I've had a long career painting. Maybe it's time to try something else."

"We won't stop looking for a cure." Strength radiated in Thomas's voice as he scooped a protective arm around Maggie.

"Good God, Thomas, what happened to your face?" Sophie leaned forward and squinted at him.

"I'm okay. Starting to feel better already."

"So, what do we do?" Erin asked.

A tired smile played across Maggie's lips. "Well, first let's lay some ground rules. Absolutely no feeling sorry for me. I have seen more sights in this marvelous world than most of the population could ever hope to see. I have seen my darling girls grow to be strong, intelligent, beautiful women." She gazed thoughtfully at Nikki. "It would be nice to see my first grandchild."

Nikki gave her a faint smile. "Now you're sounding like Dylan. Let me get through the wedding, then we'll see what we can do."

"Fair enough. And there's to be no asking me if I'm okay all the time. I have had a little cold lately and I've been tired, but that doesn't have anything to do with anything. Let's just all consider that I'm fine unless I let you know otherwise. This is only affecting my eyesight. I'm still as healthy as I've ever been and expect to continue that way."

She drew a deep breath and looked long at each of them, as though she were memorizing their faces. "I'm okay with this. I want all of you to be okay, too."

Nikki nodded and squeezed her mother's hand. Erin rose and hugged her. Nikki did the same when Erin was through and Thomas held on to Maggie through it all.

The upset and confusion swirling in Tess's stomach settled and she sat back in her chair. The love they all shared was a tangible thing, binding them all together. And whether they realized it or not, the love between Maggie and Thomas was an awe-inspiring force.

Somehow, someway, they would get through this. Maggie would be all right.

A feeling of comfort stole over Tess, along with a new determination. They all deserved happiness in this life. The one thing she'd learned from watching her mother was that happiness didn't always come to you. Sometimes you had to go out and snatch a little happiness for yourself.

She was going to need all the happiness she could find to help her deal with this new twist in her life, and if she had to go out and get it she would. She'd call Mason. Somehow, she'd make him see that they should be together.

16

For the millionth time that day, Mason pulled his thoughts from Tess and her family and focused on the setting around him. A country music song he didn't recognize twanged from a jukebox in the old diner. The scents of coffee and bacon filled the air as the clink of silverware, clank of dishes and murmur of voices filtered through the strains of the song.

Uncle Gabe, his mother's brother, sipped at his coffee. "I'm really glad you called, Mason. It's been way too long. So, how is everything?"

"Well, not too good, to be honest."

He wasn't sure why he'd called his uncle. Somehow, it just seemed time to get back in touch with his real family. He took a sip of his own coffee and nearly scalded his tongue. That was par for the course.

"Yeah, well, from what you said on the phone, you can't blame this woman of yours for being upset."

"I'm sure she is."

Gabe's eyebrows rose. "What do you mean you're sure she is? Haven't you spoken to her?"

"I tried. I couldn't get through. I went over once and banged on the door, but no one answered. Besides, what would be the point?"

"To tell her you're sorry for being a pigheaded fool. How could you have asked them to leave like that?"

Frustration welled up inside Mason. He shook his head. "We'd just had all that trouble with Rafe. He's one of the kids from Project Mentor. All I could think about was that we were going to lose our best shot at getting the youth center up and running. I lost my head. I guess I panicked."

"Jeez."

"I know it was a stupid, idiotic thing to do and I regret the hell out of it, but it's done. I can't take it back."

"You're damn right you can't take it back, but you sure as hell can apologize."

Mason stared at his uncle. How many times had he rehearsed that apology in his head? "It wouldn't matter. Look, you don't understand."

"Try me."

Mason gripped his coffee cup. "It was never meant to last. Our relationship was doomed from the start. I was a fool to let myself get involved with her." He gritted his teeth as memories of his first meeting with Tess flashed through his mind. "I just…couldn't help myself. It's complicated."

Gabe's eyes narrowed as he settled back in the booth, cradling his coffee cup. "I don't have to be anywhere."

"Tess is not the settling-down type."

My relationships with men do tend to be temporary.

Gabe blew on his coffee, then took another sip. "I never would have pegged you for a quitter, Mason."

Mason took a deep breath before responding. "I asked her to live with me. I meant it. I knew she wasn't ready for more. I don't know that I was, but I wanted to share my life with her." He paused. "She wasn't ready even for that."

"So, she needed a little time."

"I don't think so. I was getting in too deep. Don't you see it's better this way?"

"No, I don't see. You say you're in love with that girl. I'll bet she made a real difference in your life. Look at you now. When was the last time you got a decent night's sleep? How can this be better?"

"I'm cutting my losses, okay?"

"That's a bunch of crap."

Anger and resentment rose in Mason. "Look, it hurts." He shook his head. "Is it such a bad thing that I don't want to keep being left behind?"

"She didn't just leave you, you know," Gabe said softly.

Mason's gaze locked with his uncle's.

"Your mother, she was my sister before she had you. She left us all and it hurt me, too." He shrugged. "Granted, losing a sister can't really compare to losing a mother, but I felt that loss as much as you did."

Mason stared at his coffee. "I don't like to talk about her."

"It wasn't you she was leaving. It was your father. You think your Uncle Al's a hardhead. Where do you think he learned to be so uncompromising? And you don't think the drinking started after she left?"

Gabe shook his head. "That had started long before. Hell, I encouraged her to leave him and you would have, too, had you been old enough to understand what was really going on. But, Mason, I swear to God it never occurred to me that she would leave you, too."

"That was a long time ago. There's no point in re-hashing it all."

"There is if you're still carrying around that wound."

"Uncle Gabe, I know you mean well, but this isn't necessary. I'm fine. I'm all grown up and I get that bad things happen to good people."

"That's right, son. You're good people and bad things did happen to you, but you don't have to keep suffering for it. You've paid your dues. It's time for you to quit being afraid of being hurt and to take that risk and grab it all."

Mason stared at his uncle, and he wanted to cringe at the truth in his words. He'd run away from happiness to keep from getting hurt. He met his uncle's gaze and nodded. "You're right. It's time I took a risk."

"Hi." Tess nodded at Mason as he stood in her door-way. Her pulse quickened in anticipation.

"Hi." His eyebrows drew together and apprehension rippled off him. "Thanks for agreeing to see me."

"I'm glad you called. I was actually going to call you."

"Really? To tell me I'm a pigheaded idiot?"

"Well, since you already know that…" She shrugged.

"So, can I come in?"

"No."

"No?"

She shook her head. "Let's go out."

"Out?"

"Yep, you know, sky, fresh air."

"Right, I think I remember that." He shuffled aside and let her move past him, then fell into step beside her. "Where is it that we're going?"

She smiled what she hoped was a mysterious smile. "It's a surprise."

"And will I like this surprise?"

"Oh, I certainly hope so." She pulled her keys from her purse as they neared the parking lot. "We'll take my car."

They reached her car and he held the door for her. She savored his familiar scent as she slid past him into the driver's seat.

"Okay," he said as he settled beside her in the passenger's seat. "I'm ready."

She drove with the windows down, in spite of the slight coolness in the air. "Don't you like the wind in your hair?" she asked as they turned onto the interstate and picked up speed.

"Tess, there's something that I really need to say to you."

"No, not yet. I have something to say to you, too, but let's wait until we get to where we're going."

She turned on the radio and tuned in her favorite rock station. Mason blew out a breath in an apparent effort to relax, if the tension spiking off him was any indication. She glanced at him, grinning as they neared their destination.

"Oh, no." He shook his head, even as a hesitant smile curved his lips. "I should have known."

"You know you enjoyed it the last time."

She parked along a quiet side street, then turned to him, excitement rippling up her spine. "Ready?"

"I am if you are."

A salty breeze hit her as she exited the car. The rumble of the surf sounded from beyond the row of buildings in front of them. Mason crossed to her side and they headed silently along the street to a trail leading to the shore. They picked their way over the sand until the Atlantic lay before them, calmer today than it had been on their last visit.

His gaze narrowed on her as they reached a spot in the sand not far from the breaking surf. "Are we going for a swim?"

"In all our clothes?"

"Didn't stop us last time."

"It's early November. Could be chilly. Do you want to?"

His shoulders moved in an easy shrug. "I do if you want to."

"Let's sit for a while. I just wanted to feel the sun on my face."

He nodded and they settled together, side by side in the sand. Gulls screeched overhead and the crash of the surf lulled them into a comfortable silence. Tess leaned back and breathed deeply of the sea air. Suddenly it seemed she had all the time in the world. Time to discover who she was.

Time to love a great love.

Mason shifted beside her, brushing sand from his hands. "So, about what I wanted to say before…"

She took a deep breath and faced him. "Okay, I'm listening."

"Tess…first and foremost I want to apologize. Asking you and your family to leave that night was unforgivable."

"You did what you felt was right at the time, given the circumstances."

His eyes widened and surprise flickered through him.

"I was upset to think we might be losing our shot at the youth center."

"I know."

"All I could think of was Rafe lying in that hospital bed and all the other kids that might end up like him if we didn't get the center going."

"I know. How is he?"

A slow smile curved his lips. "He's doing great. That kid has the world's hardest head. He's frustrated as hell that he can't move around like he used to, but it's temporary and he's managing. He said he saw you the other day."

"I did stop by. And how is his father?"

"Holding steady. I think he's trying his best to get healthy so he can make things up to Rafe. He's been clean for almost eight months now."

She nodded. "I'm glad."

"You must think I'm the biggest prick for turning my nose up at your aunt and her readings."

"It's hard to accept something you don't quite understand. Maybe you should have her do a reading for you, so you can see what it's all about. I'd love to hear what she has to say."

"Sounds a little intimidating, but if it'll get me back in her good graces, I'll give it a try."

"It's pretty hard to fall out of Aunt Sophie's good graces. I have never met a more patient or understanding person. She writes all this off to everyone's life lessons.

"She told me you called her. That was nice." She ran her fingers through the sand. "You know, she doesn't judge you for what happened."

"And do you?"

Tess glanced away, toward the water where a gull

dipped low over the swells. "I did. It was hard not to. Hard not to be hurt." She turned back to him. "You see, no one has ever rejected me. Ever. Not in my entire life. I didn't know how to deal with that."

"Tess, I'm so sorry. I hope you know it wasn't you I was rejecting."

"It's okay. I needed that. I needed to know what it feels like to be normal."

His eyes crinkled as he laughed. "You, my dear, will never be normal."

"It isn't funny. I can be as normal as the next person."

"Sweetheart, I believe you can be anything you set your mind to, but you're special in a way I can't begin to describe. And I completely understand why you need to be on your own. I don't think I had thought through all I might have been asking when I asked you to live with me. I guess I was thinking of myself, trying to hold on to something that wasn't mine to hold on to." He paused and held her gaze. "I'm really sorry for that."

She reached over and took his hand, needing the connection. A peace he hadn't possessed before hummed quietly below his surface. She cocked her head and let her gaze drift over him. "You've changed."

Surprise rounded his eyes. "How?"

"You're more at peace."

"Yeah, maybe so. I've done a lot of thinking since the gala. Had a long talk with my uncle Gabe. He helped me put things in perspective. It would be nice if you could meet him."

He turned her hand over in his and traced circles along her palm. "Anyway, I'm a pigheaded fool and why you agreed to see me and why you're being so damn understanding I can barely fathom, but I have never been so grateful for anything in my entire life. Thank you for seeing me and for hearing me out. It means the world to me."

She closed her eyes and let his bittersweet longing wash over her. He did mean to let her go—leave her for good to allow her to move on to whatever new love might be out there waiting for her.

But was she ready to leave?

"Do you believe that we each have one great love?" she asked.

He patted her hand, then let it go. "I don't know. I guess it's nice to think so."

"Nikki believes it. Her whole childhood she wanted our mother to quit roaming from lover to lover and settle down with her true love."

"And did she?"

"Not yet, but I think we're going to figure that one out soon."

"What about Nikki? Is Dylan her great love?"

"Oh, yes. The two are practically inseparable. She said she knew it the moment she met him, but she was so afraid of losing him that she hid the truth, even from herself, until she nearly lost him."

"I think I can relate to that whole hanging-on thing."

A sailboat appeared on the horizon, tacking slowly to the north. He watched it for a few minutes, then turned back to her. "I'm glad Nikki and Dylan were able to work things out."

"Yeah, so maybe she was right. Maybe there is one great love for each of us." She squinted into the sun as it peeped from behind a cloud. "I think maybe I would like it if that were so."

He nodded and his gaze darkened. "I think I would, too."

"Well, you know there's one way we might be able to find out if we each have a true love."

"How?"

"We could pretend that I never turned down your proposal to live with you." Her heart thudded as his eyebrows drew together.

"Tess, what are you saying?"

"I'm saying that I was afraid when you first asked me. My identity was all tied up in being a sexual healer. I was afraid that if I stayed with you I'd lose that identity. I had no idea who I was outside of that role. It was hard to get over that, but I've been figuring out who I am. I've been working with the teens."

"I heard about your nature walk. The kids think you're all that."

She nodded. "I do believe we could each have one great love and I think that maybe…quite possibly…it could be that my one great love is you."

Dismay and joy swirled out from him in a cloud of confusion. "Tess."

She frowned when he didn't continue. "I tell you I think you may be my one great love and that's all you have to say?"

"I don't know what to say. You've taken me completely by surprise." Those adorable dimples of his made an appearance as he raised his hands in appeal. "I had hoped you might accept my apology. This is beyond my greatest expectation."

A giggle tickled its way up her throat and trickled out of her mouth. "So, why don't you kiss me and tell me you think that maybe I might possibly be your one great love, too?"

"I'm sorry. I don't think I can do that."

"You can't?"

He shook his head, his expression solemn. "No, I'm afraid not."

She pulled away, frowning. "Oh."

"You see, there is no 'maybe' about it. I do have one great love and there is absolutely no doubt in my mind that that love is you."

"Oh." She smiled. "So."

"So." He leaned in toward her and she met him halfway, but just when his lips parted, a hairbreadth away from hers, he scooped her up, then stood.

"Mason, what are you doing?" She wrapped her arms around his neck as he jostled her into a more comfortable position.

"Coloring outside of the lines."

"Oh?"

Those marvelous dimples flashed at her again, and she laughed as he ran with her to the water. Gulls screeched overhead and white foam broke around them when he dove with her into the surf.

The waves closed over them in a chilling rush and Tess slipped free to swim several long strokes before surfacing beside Mason. He frowned and tucked a stray strand of her hair behind her ear as they treaded water just beyond the breaking waves.

"Cold?" he asked.

She nodded. "Freezing."

He wrapped his arms around her, while kicking to keep them afloat. "So, if you move in with me and miracle of all miracles you decide that I am after all your one great love, then what does that mean for your gift?"

"Actually, I'm not sure."

"Would it mean that you lose the gift?"

"It might."

He pushed back from her. "Tess…that's not right. I could never ask you to do that."

"Well, you're not asking me."

"It's too big a sacrifice."

She kicked forward, closing the gap between them. "If it is a sacrifice, which I'm not so sure it is—the gift could evolve in a way—then it's my sacrifice to make." She draped first one, then her other arm over his shoulders. "And I want to make it."

Deep grooves formed between his eyebrows and his eyes glittered. "Are you sure?"

"Absolutely."

He kissed her then, his mouth hungry for hers as the warmth of his love blanketed her. She pressed her body close to his and kicked with him as they bobbed in the water with the sun warming them and the breeze wrapping around them.

When at last he pulled away, desire shone in his dark eyes. His gaze drifted over her. "Are you ready to go home?"

"Yes."

His mouth quirked to one side. "But what about all your male friends? I hate to admit it, but I can't help feeling jealous when they're always with you."

"Believe it or not, they haven't been hanging around much since I met you."

"Really? And are you okay with not having them there all the time? Would you be okay with having just some of them around some of the time?"

She gazed past him to the lone sail now far away on the horizon. "I don't need all that fuss around me anymore. After the gala I spent some time alone and I think I've got a good start on who I am just by myself."

"And who are you, Tess McClellan?"

"I'm an independent female with a penchant for a good time and a desire to give back to my community. I've discovered that I like to read and take long walks and it is possible for me to order just one item off a menu. I know that simply put I can not only be alone, but that I actually enjoy being alone at times. But most of all…I'm happy." She smiled. "That's who I am."

"Well, I think you sound like the person I want to spend a lot of time with."

"Good. So, who are you?"

"Me?" He pointed to himself. "Who am I?"

She nodded and smiled to encourage him.

"Ah, I've got it. I'm a man who's learned to listen to the woman he loves."

"Yeah?"

"Got that straight."

"Okay, so we need to talk about a plan. We need some goals here."

He cocked his head. "You mean a life plan?"

"Right, one we can start on right after I finish ravaging you."

"You're going to ravage me?"

"Don't worry, you're going to love it. Have I ever steered you wrong?"

"I'm listening. Just tell me what you want me to do. I am yours to command."

She smiled and let the sun dance across her wet skin, her heart filled to bursting as they headed back to the shore. "Then take me home, so I can have my way with you."

"And that life plan?" he asked as he lifted her from the water.

Secure in his arms, she traced the curve of his cheek. "I stick with you, for good, because you're the one and only man that I can handle."

* * * * *

Watch for the conclusion of Dorie Graham's
SEXUAL HEALING *series*
with Erin's story FAKING IT
Coming October 2005 from Harlequin Blaze

HARLEQUIN®
Blaze™

COMING NEXT MONTH

#207 OPEN INVITATION? Karen Kendall
The Man-Handlers, Bk. 3

He's a little rough around the edges. In fact, Lilia London has no idea how to polish Dan Granger. With only a few weeks to work, she has no time to indulge the steamy attraction between them. But he's so sexy when he's persistent. Maybe she'll indulge... just a little.

#208 FAKING IT Dorie Graham
Sexual Healing, Bk. 3

What kind of gift makes men sick? Erin McClellan doesn't have the family talent for sexual healing. So she's sworn off guys...until she meets the tempting Jack Langston. When he's still strong the next morning, she wants to hit those sheets one more time!

#209 PRIVATE RELATIONS Nancy Warren
Do Not Disturb

PR director Kit Prescott is throwing a Fantasy Weekend Contest to promote Hush—Manhattan's hottest boutique hotel. The first winner is sexy, single—and her ex-fiancé, Peter Garson! How can Kit entertain the man who's never stopped starring in all *her* fantasies?

#210 TALKING ABOUT SEX... Vicki Lewis Thompson

Engineer Jess Harkins has always had a thing for Katie Peterson. He could even have been her first lover...if he'd had the nerve to take her up on her offer. Now Katie's an opinionated shock jock who obviously hasn't forgiven him, given the way she's killing his latest project over the airwaves. So what can Jess do but teach her to put her mouth to better use?

#211 CAN'T GET ENOUGH Sarah Mayberry

Being stuck in an elevator can do strange things to people. And Claire Marsden should know. The hours she spent with archrival Jack Brook resulted in the hottest sex she's ever had! She'd love to forget the whole thing...if only she didn't want to do it again.

#212 POSSESSION Tori Carrington
Dangerous Liaisons, Bk. 1

When FBI agent Akela Brooks returns home to New Orleans, she never expects to end up as a hostage of Claude Lafitte, the accused Quarter killer—or to enjoy her captivity so much. She immediately knows the sexy Cajun is innocent of murder. But for Akela, that doesn't make him any less dangerous....

HBCNM0905